"Once I started I couldn't put it down."

—Joshilyn Jackson, *New York Times* bestselling author

"The characters in *Invisible as Air* are so real, so flawed, so compelling and vulnerable. With her trademark wit and honesty, even in the face of sorrow, Fishman will take you on a journey you won't soon forget."

—Greer Hendricks, *New York Times* bestselling author

For *Inheriting Edith*

"A heartbreaking story about life, love, and friendship that you'll want to devour in one sitting."

—Erin Duffy, author of *Regrets Only*

"A beautifully crafted story about second chances and about life's big surprises. Warm spirited and emotionally rich, *Inheriting Edith* celebrates the fine line between friendship and family. These characters will tug at your heart."

—Jamie Brenner, author of *Gilt*

"I loved this compelling and achingly real novel about friendship, family, and second chances."

—Jillian Cantor, author of *Half Life*

THE Fun Widow's BOOK TOUR

Also by Zoe Fishman

Invisible as Air
Inheriting Edith
Driving Lessons
Saving Ruth
Balancing Acts

THE Fun Widow's BOOK TOUR

A NOVEL

ZOE FISHMAN

wm

WILLIAM MORROW

An Imprint of HarperCollins*Publishers*

P.S.™ is a trademark of HarperCollins Publishers.

HarperCollins books may be purchased for educational, business, or sales promotional use. For information, please email the Special Markets Department at SPsales@harpercollins.com.

FIRST EDITION

Designed by Diahann Sturge

Book illustration art © StockSmartStart / Shutterstock

Library of Congress Cataloging-in-Publication Data has been applied for.

ISBN 978-0-06-283824-7

23 24 25 26 27 LBC 5 4 3 2 1

For my Zoedies

CHAPTER 1

It was the same dream, every time. Mia's husband walked through their front door in his short-sleeve button-down and tie and told her that he was leaving her for someone else.

In the dream, the new girlfriend was pregnant.

Mia watched her, the woman who had replaced her. From a distance, always.

Until last night. The girlfriend was short and pear-shaped, both things that Mia was not. Her hair was dreadlocked. She made her own milk out of nuts and was showing Mia how in her dirty kitchen.

Mia did not care about making milk out of nuts.

They fought.

"How can you live with yourself?" Mia had screamed at her. "He has two sons!"

The girlfriend had volunteered that perhaps she and Mia's husband could visit and explain. Mia had jumped from the stool she had been perched on and put her hands around the girlfriend's pale and sweaty neck, her dreads scratching Mia's wrists.

It had been two years and nine months since her husband had died.

Recently, Mia had decided to try out his side of the bed. This was for two reasons: she was worried that the mattress would become lopsided and also she had gotten an ear-cartilage piercing instead of a tattoo and it really, really hurt. Mia couldn't sleep on her right side anymore, even though that was the way she had been sleeping her whole forty-three years of life.

She had wanted a tattoo, but after the tattoo lady told Mia that her husband's handwriting was too small to replicate and that in a few years' time it would bleed and become illegible, the piercing had seemed like the next best thing. Mia hadn't anticipated that the piercer would literally be plunging a spear through her ear, however. It had been a far cry from the gun they had used at Claire's when she was nine.

The pain had been excruciating and shocking. Like childbirth but much, much quicker. Eleven months later, and it still oozed and throbbed.

Her phone alarm sounded, and Mia toggled it to off, blinding herself in the process. Next door, she could hear the soft rustling of her eight-year-old son. Downstairs, the faint whir of her five-year-old's sound machine as he slept. The coffee machine sighed dramatically from the kitchen as it rumbled to life.

Early morning. Five A.M. Mia's writing time. Or at least it was supposed to be. She rubbed her eyes and considered the dream. A white woman with dreads, of all things.

She hauled herself up to a seated position, wincing as her bones and joints argued with her decision. Mia could not imagine feeling older, but of course she would. Well, not of course. She understood that now.

She sat on her toilet at an angle because she couldn't fit otherwise. It was a charming house, their house, but it was old and had belonged to a tiny married couple who had lived inside of it for forty-some-odd years with two angry dogs and an array of spindly cats before Mia and her husband had bought it. Their first house—the worst house in the best neighborhood, as they had been taught to seek.

It had been a year of looking, mostly by Mia with their sons in tow while her husband was at work; her biceps at Linda Hamilton in *Terminator* level because of the constant toting of their very sturdy younger child in his detachable infant car seat from room to uninspiring room as their older ran through each house, checking closets and longingly admiring toys he was forbidden to touch.

Mia could glean so much about a family from their home while they were out. What was disheartening to her was the fact that no one in the dozens of homes she perused appeared to read. There was not a book to be found, not even on a bedside table, and as an author herself, this was especially painful.

Mia had boxes and boxes of curated books, and she had lugged them from apartment to apartment during her thirteen-year tenure in New York and then from New York to their new rental home in New Jersey in a truck that had arrived one week late, in the dead of summer, when only the mosquitoes moved.

In the spring, three years later, when their beleaguered but loyal real estate agent had led them inside the house they would buy, Mia had grabbed her husband's hand with her free one and squeezed it. Beyond the Technicolor-painted walls, pet hair–encrusted carpeting, and thimble-size bathrooms, there was a black-and-white-tiled kitchen filled with the very specific love for food and cooking that Mia did not naturally possess but wanted to. They had bought it at a shocking deal for the neighborhood; it had been a miracle, really. And then they had painted the walls a color they both agreed on called "Agreeable Gray" and ripped up the carpeting to reveal beautiful wood floors and moved in.

And then.

Mia grabbed her washcloth now, ran very cold water over it, and then plunged her face inside its folds. She brushed her teeth. She did not look in the mirror. It was cruel what grief did to one's face, especially the eyes. All of Mia's tears had taken a toll that creams and concealers could not disguise. But still, she tried.

She slipped her favorite gray sweatshirt from its hanger and zipped it all the way up, pulling its generous hood over her head. A tent of concentration, giant mug of coffee with a glug of half-and-half poured in, her glasses, her laptop. These were her tools.

Don't pull up your email, don't pull up your email, don't pull up your email, you're supposed to be writing! Mia chanted to herself as she pulled up her email. "Virtual Book Tour," the subject line read.

Her book, a memoir of her life after losing her husband, would be released into the world today, even though she had finished copy editing the fourth round of rewrites a year before. The time it took for a book to be born was glacial in a world where you could order printer ink at midnight and find it on your doorstep the next morning.

Before a book was a book, it was a galley. A galley was a much cheaper version of the book, printed before final edits were made, and its purpose was to garner reviews from book bloggers who in turn would encourage their voracious reading fans to preorder, all with the goal of turning the book into a bestseller and thus the author into a financial success, because publishing was a business, and businesses needed to make money.

Mia had known this at first in a tangential way, but five books later she knew it in a very personal way. If her books didn't make money, she didn't earn out her advance, and if she didn't earn out her advance, her career was in jeopardy. Best-case scenario was that her next advance would remain the same. Worst case was that there was no next advance; there was no next book. It was a constant roller coaster for her, one tied to her heart.

She was a good writer, but was she good enough? With each book, she climbed another rung of the proverbial ladder to success. And by *success,* Mia meant two things: she would be able to support her family, and she would debut on the *New York Times* bestseller list. It was a very long ladder.

Her galley had been mailed all over the country to every book blogger on the block by her publicist's assistant, who likely was paid less an hour than a Trader Joe's cashier and lived in Queens with three roommates in a one-bedroom apartment while bartending at night. Authors made no money, but publishing assistants *really* made no money.

Starting today, and for three weeks thereafter, a different blogger would post their review of Mia's memoir. This was what they called a tour now, Mia guessed. She had only one in-person reading at her beloved bookstore in town, and Mia had arranged that herself.

This was standard practice, although the general reading public always assumed otherwise. It was part of the facade, created by movies and reality television stars promoting books that they had most certainly not written themselves. They got the book tours because actual humans showed up. And bestselling authors too, the big guns whose names everybody knew—they got them. But the mid-listers like herself? Forget it.

Mia couldn't blame her publisher, really. Her first book, about a group of women in a yoga class in Brooklyn, had been a smash, and she had somehow wormed her way into a business-class ticket to the Frankfurt Book Fair, where she had been whisked from booze-laden party to booze-laden party and signed copies in a freezing conference hall the size of twenty football fields. None of her book sales since had compared, hence the tour that wasn't a tour at all. Again.

Mia pulled the strings of her sweatshirt hood tighter, so that now only her glasses and nose were visible.

Books and Dogs; Book Junkie; Book Babe; Rabid Reader; Words and Turds—these were just a few of the blogs with which her memoir's fate resided.

"Oh, come on, Book Babe, don't be a Book Bitch," Mia whispered as she clicked the link. She had been reviewed hundreds of times before, but those reviews were of her fiction, of characters and plots that she had created out of nothing. This time, the reviews would be of her. Because it was a memoir.

They had to be nice, right? The author was a young widow with two sons. She had endured sudden tragedy and still she stood, still she wrote, and wasn't that something to be praised for? Mia took a deep breath and then she read.

I wanted to like this book, I really did, Book Babe had typed in purple font.

"Oh fuck," said Mia.

But where was the author? A memoir is supposed to be about the person writing the book, yes? Sure, her to-do lists are hers, but where is her emotional journey? It's all about keeping her sons happy and tracking their feelings like a sniper, but what about her own? I finished the book with no idea who she was, where she is now, or where she's going. Bleh. Two out of five stars.

"Fuck you, you fucking fuck," Mia growled as tears sprang to her eyes.

Book Babe probably had a partner who was alive and maybe one kid, a baby who went down for a two-hour nap after lunch so she could beach-wave her hair. Mia sneered at Book Babe's photo before slamming her laptop shut.

"He was forty-four and he left for work one morning and never came back," Mia said to her empty room. "I'm still here. He's not. His story is my story, you idiot."

Mia took off her glasses and rubbed her eyes. The truth was that she knew what Book Babe was saying because she had heard it before, from her editor.

This is a heartbreaking story of loss, her editor had written in her letter, the letter that came as an email attachment three weeks after Mia had turned in the first draft of her memoir. *I love the idea and the first thirty pages, but the rest needs some work.* In book speak, *needs some work* meant *start over.* It was the editorial equivalent of *bless your heart.*

It was hard to hear *start over* when Mia had spent thirteen months writing her first draft, but to say that she was surprised would have been a lie. She'd written it right after her husband had died, oscillating from the page to her sons to the horrid business of dismantling his life and then back again. Of course it *needed some work.*

She had called her agent to commiserate, but her agent had agreed with her editor.

"There's no you here, Mia," she had told her. "It's all about him."

"Because he is me! That's the world I'm living in right now," Mia had replied. "He's gone and I'm here and I don't want anyone to forget him. It's a memoir of not surviving, not a memoir of, like, me being chubby in middle school."

"You were chubby in middle school?"

Mia had hung up the phone.

She hadn't changed her memoir's focus because she hadn't wanted to—it was the first time in her career that she had stood her ground after dozens of title changes and point-of-view shifts and turning her beloved em dashes into commas over a ten-year span. Mia wanted to write her husband back to life, just for a little bit; she would figure out herself later.

Next door, two size-four boy feet hit the wood floor with a

thud, rattling the ceramic vase filled with pencils, pens, a pair of scissors, and a rainbow ruler on Mia's desk.

"Hi, Mom," her elder said, shuffling into her room, reminding Mia exactly of Bugs Bunny with his naked stick-legs and long, skinny feet.

His father's feet.

"Hi, buddy," said Mia, taking him into her lap even though he was just shy of being too big for it.

Downstairs, her younger hit the ground with a thud of his own and ran to fling open his door.

"Mom!" he yelled from below.

"Morning!" Mia yelled back.

"Did you have a good sleep?" he yelled, taking the stairs loudly. *Boom. Boom. Boom.* Her elder smiled up at her. His dark hair smelled like roses.

"I did," she said.

A LOT OF people seemed to think that Mia turned in her manuscript one week and then after a team of Keebler Elves ran it through a giant printer and bound the pages with ribbons of tree sap, it appeared.

That wasn't how it worked. Every writer seemed to have their own system, but Mia's went like this: synopsis; outline; and submittal of her official first draft—she had two unofficial drafts that would never see the light of day—to her agent and editor simultaneously. Mia was not a critique-group kind of writer because she didn't like too many cooks in her kitchen.

After her submission, Mia still had another two rounds of revisions to go until the manuscript was perceived as something people might actually want to read, and then came the line editing, the copy editing, the marketing pitch, the publicity push, the galley, and then and only then: a real-life book.

Back in the olden days, when Mia had a husband to help with their sons and even going back as far as the Mesozoic Age of her career, before she was married and all she had to worry about was herself, it would take Mia around nine or ten months, give or take, to write a book. Her memoir had taken her double that time.

The only way she had been able to do it was with her best girlfriends' help. She had three of them: Chelsea, Rachel, and George. They were not a package deal; they were from three very different and specific phases of Mia's life: Chelsea from her childhood in a suburb of Atlanta, Rachel from college in Boston, and George from post-college/early-twenties Manhattan.

Each of them had taken turns coming once a month and banished her to the garage while they entertained, fed, and bathed the dudes—a moniker Rachel had come up with—with limitless patience and affection.

It was the kindest act Mia had ever witnessed, much less been on the receiving end of. She had a father and she had her in-laws, but they had all been and still were grieving too, too filled with sadness to be selfless.

Mia's mother had died from pancreatic cancer when Mia was thirty-six, which should have prepared Mia for the death of her husband but hadn't. The difference, and Mia had thought about this a lot, was that she had gotten to say goodbye to her mother.

She hadn't gotten to tell her husband goodbye, to tell him how lucky she had felt to be his wife. He was just gone.

Then again, she had also had to accept the fact that her father had married a woman named Judy less than two years after her mother had died, a woman whom he had met in the fish aisle at Petco.

People said all the time to Mia, *You can't make this up!* when she was cognizant enough to tell them about the last ten years of her life and Mia always thought, *Yes, you can make it up, but I wouldn't unless I really hated my protagonist.*

During the eighteen months it had taken Mia to write her memoir, her brain had felt like a punching bag: her editor was right; no, Mia was right; *Less him and more of you!; No, more him, who cares about you!* In the end, her memoir was half prose and half prescription. Mia had wanted it to be called *The New Widow's Guide to the Uncharted Hellscape of Your New Life,* but her editor had insisted on *New York Minute* because Mia and her husband had met on the F train.

The book could never have been about Mia. If she put her husband down on paper, he would never really be gone; that was her thinking, and it was true. But writing it as a single parent had also nearly killed her: exhaustion and grief as a package deal will fuck you up, Mia had learned. She had even gone to the doctor halfway through, thinking she was dying.

"Healthy as a horse," her doctor had informed her over email when her blood tests had come back.

Mia realized now that she probably should have included that anecdote in the memoir—that would have been a personal detail about her tangential demise—but she hadn't. And now here she was, reading the very same criticism she'd willfully ignored from the start. It wasn't a great sign for sales.

Mia sighed and stood up. Time to put the house back in order for the day that had already begun. Morning was a shitshow in their house: soggy cereal and walks to school, kisses on both cheeks from her younger as she said goodbye, breathing finally in the quiet of daybreak. Then back home; coffee at the counter as she begrudgingly read the news: disaster, death, corruption—*Oh look, a salmon recipe!*; back upstairs to clean out her inbox and then make the beds; do the dishes; plan dinner; scrub the toothpaste from the sink; pay the bills; call the roofer about the crack that never stopped leaking no matter what; retrieve the dudes; drive them to practices; feed and water them; and then, only then: sleep. Her favorite part of the day was closing the blinds.

Mia made her own bed, she never didn't think of her husband when she made the bed that had been theirs once and was now just her own, and then made her elder's, reveling in the still-sweet smell of him on his sheets.

She had updated his room with a new blue-and-white-striped duvet, tossing the old, faded, *babyish* one. So many artifacts of their lives together as a family of four were being replaced: most recently a bigger couch, since the dudes kept growing and growing.

Their original couch was one that Mia had purchased with a large chunk of the advance from her first book, right after she and her husband had gotten engaged. She had been so mad, dropping all that money herself in an overpriced furniture shop in SoHo.

Her husband—her fiancé then—hadn't been able to split the cost; he hadn't even offered. As a Ph.D. candidate, he was perpetually broke, something that had always bothered her slightly but really worried her in that furniture shop. There was the promise of his degree bringing in money down the line, but just how far down was it? And the loans. Mia had just come to terms with the fact that his college loans would be hers too, once they were married.

She had been thinking about all this as the trim salesman, dressed in pants so tight they verged on obscene, rang her up.

"What's the matter with you?" her husband had asked Mia on the cobblestoned street afterward.

"I just dropped like three thousand dollars," she had complained.

"So? We need a new couch, it's good quality, it was on sale," he replied. It was summer, and his forehead had been sweating, tiny beads all across it, like braille.

"When have you ever spent that much money on something?" she had spit back.

He had looked down at the ring finger on her left hand.

"Oh," Mia had said, feeling like an asshole.

He had made her a sharer, her husband. Of course her money would be his money because his money, however little he had of it, had always been hers. It was there on her ring finger, sparkling up at her. It was in the dinners he prepared, the beers and cigarettes he passed to her at parties—the way he invited everyone he knew everywhere he went.

Mia had never been good at sharing—her father always retold

the story of her first playdate, when she ran into his room sobbing because the friend she had invited over was *touching her toys*—but her husband had changed that.

He had changed so much about Mia for the better. Her former self, the her before him, was a fossil now, buried deep underground. But what about her current self? The her after him?

Who the hell was she now?

CHAPTER 2

HAPPY PUB DAY, @MIAMACHER76! HER PUBLI-
cist proclaimed on Twitter.

So happy this beautiful book is in the world @MiaMacher76, her
agent Instagrammed.

*This memoir will make you laugh and cry. Thank you @Mia
Macher76,* her editor wrote on Facebook. She was quoting a reviewer
but had kindly left out the end of that sentence: *but mostly cry.*

That reviewer had said her book was too sad. International
publishers were saying her book was too niche, which was a problem because authors needed to have their books translated and
published abroad if they ever were to have even a modicum of
hope about earning out and receiving royalties down the line.

New widows don't have time to read, an Italian publisher had
told her agent.

"But what about Sheryl Sandberg's book?" Mia had asked her
agent anyway. "That thing was on the bestseller list for years."

"You're not Sheryl Sandberg," her agent had retorted.

Mia closed her computer and stared morosely at the blue mug

of coffee on her desk. *Let That Shit Go,* it told her in white block letters, and man, was that easier said than done.

Mia's desk was in her bedroom. It hadn't always been—back when she shared her bed with her husband, her desk had been shoved into a corner in the foyer—but now it sat right next to her bed, because why not? Nothing else was going on in her bedroom.

A short stack of folders flanked the left corner of the desk, one labeled "Stuff," one labeled "Book," and one labeled "101" for the creative writing class she taught at the community center. A yellow notebook filled with to-do list after to-do list sat on the right corner, on top of a black-and-white composition notebook with "Bills" scrawled across its front in black Sharpie. There was also her red planner, in which she dutifully recorded everything the three of them had to do in her minuscule handwriting. The dudes' stuff was in green ink, and hers was in black. Single parenting was the Organizational Olympics, and Mia had the gold.

Her desk sat in front of two large windows. Tree branches dotted her view, bare and brown in the winter; budding with pink, yellow, and white blooms in the spring; endlessly green in the summer; and on fire with red, yellow, and orange in the fall. Below her was the worn gravel street and her neighbors' two-story homes, all more or less replicas of her own.

The worst house in the best neighborhood: she and her husband had found it.

To the left of the desk, on the gray wainscoted wall, hung a sign. *Buck up, Buttercup,* it proclaimed in bold font, with beautifully painted scarlet-, marigold-, celadon-, and salmon-colored flowers crowding its borders. Mia had been with her husband and the dudes when she saw it at a tiny shop in town. They had been running ahead of her, their younger on her husband's shoulders. She had bought it on the spot—it reminded Mia of her mother—and had hung it on her wall that night.

A week later, he had died.

Had her mother known? Was the sign also a sign from the beyond? It was something Mia's mother had told her since she was a whiney toddler.

Downstairs, a knock sounded. Ah, her hero: the UPS man. Every day, when Mia heard his truck rumbling down her street, she would run to the window and gaze out of it longingly. To watch him step down from his brown chariot with a box or envelope in his capable hands! For her! It was poetry in motion.

She ran down the stairs and flung open the door.

"Wha—"

"Bahhhhhhh!!!!!!"

A very happy, very bouncy female human jumped up and down in front of Mia, wielding a bottle of champagne.

"Rachel! Oh my God! What are you doing here?" Mia cried.

She grabbed Rachel, and Rachel grabbed back, sending her luggage backward and tumbling down the three stairs leading to the small porch on which they stood.

"Your bag!" said Mia.

"Oh, fuck it," said Rachel.

She unwound herself from Mia's embrace, her hair wild from the flight, her black down coat zipped up to her chin.

"Surprise!" she yelled, smiling.

"I can't believe you came!" Mia moved past her to lug the bag back up the stairs: *bump, bump, bump.*

"Believe it. Now let me in." She pushed past Mia playfully. "It's cold out here."

"Rachel, you live in Chicago. New Jersey should feel like Hawaii to you."

"Well, it doesn't," said Rachel, unzipping her jacket and handing it to Mia.

Mia squeezed it onto a hook among the ever-growing mass of the dudes' hoodies and raincoats and vests by the stained-glass front door.

"Let's release this book, motherfuckers!" Rachel yelled, waving the champagne bottle over her head.

From the first moment Mia had met Rachel, moving into their college dorm room freshman year, it was clear that Rachel knew who she was. She had walked over to Mia with her perfect posture, her regal head held high with its hundreds of braids spilling out of it like ribbons of silk, and shaken her hand.

Mia's boneless face had been streaked with tears after saying goodbye to her parents on the curb as they climbed into a cab to return home. What were they thinking, leaving her by herself? She had no idea what she was doing.

"Hey," Mia had sniffled.

"The other girls on this floor suck, so I hope you don't suck too," Rachel had said, her white Calvin Klein baby tee gleaming against her skin.

"I don't think I suck," said Mia, even though she sort of did.

Mia looked at her now, twenty-five years later, and still saw that eighteen-year-old badass. The stories of Rachel's life were etched across her face and woven through the gray strands in her hair now; they clung to her soft frame—but she was still that girl to Mia. She always would be.

"Ooh, a gallery, I love it," said Rachel, walking past the dudes' framed art on the walls. "You've really brightened up the place, Mia."

"Thanks. I went a little overboard, I know," she acknowledged as Rachel faced more of the same in the kitchen. "But, you know, the frames at IKEA are so reasonable, so?"

"Is this you?" asked Rachel, pointing to a face rendered by her five-year-old.

"It is! He gave me eyelashes."

"Good boy," said Rachel.

"I'm so happy to see you," said Mia as they both slid onto stools. "I had no idea you were coming. It wasn't on the calendar," she joked, referring to the Google Calendar that Rachel had created that first year after Mia's husband's death, when every week brought a new logistical challenge for Mia: his college loans, his car, Social Security, their healthcare, his emails, the Spotify account that she could never figure out his password to and so forever it would be him making their mixes, which had ended up being just the right blend of comforting and creepy.

Rachel had coined it the *Save Mia* Calendar, and she, George, and Chelsea had taken turns cycling through New Jersey every three months for four days at a time. Sometimes, one of them would mistake the *Save Mia* Calendar for their own, thereby alerting all of them to their Brazilian wax appointment.

"Oh lord, that calendar," said Rachel, smiling. "It's been a while."

It had been a year and a half since anyone had visited her, Mia wanted to mention but didn't. She wasn't mad about it—she understood—but she was lonely. Mia herself wasn't very good company, acknowledging that by the time the dudes were in bed and the last dish was done she could barely sit up, but she yearned for company just the same: someone to talk or not talk to in pajamas on the couch that was not one or both of her dudes. Someone who didn't need her for anything.

Before her husband had died, Mia had hated having guests—she had an undiagnosed OCD cleaning compulsion that had driven her in-laws to tears at one point—but now she craved them. Well, Rachel, George, and Chelsea specifically.

"My flight was booked five seconds after you told me your pub date," Rachel answered now. "I mean, duh. This is a big fucking deal. You wrote a memoir of the hardest year of your life during the hardest year of your life while single momming the hell out of the dudes. You deserve a parade."

A lump rose in Mia's throat. It was true, what Rachel was saying: it had been hard. It was hard. Mia didn't see it not being hard until the dudes were hopefully in college on full scholarships because how else was she going to pay for it? After that, who knew. But Mia had learned after a rash of panic attacks whenever she considered a future in which the dudes were giants and hated her to boot, because of course they would hate her, that was just what teenagers did, that she had to take life day by day.

Day by day.

"You got two flutes for the champagne?" Rachel asked, pulling her curly, dark mane back with both hands and sliding a leopard silk scrunchie off her wrist to gather it.

Mia opened the cabinet and placed the flutes on the black glossy tile of the counter.

"Why are these so dusty?" asked Rachel as she prepared to uncork the bottle.

"Ugh, fine," said Mia. She transferred them to the sink and doused the sponge with soap.

Having Rachel here, she felt almost normal. They had become best friends when their biggest worry had been how to afford MAC Spice lipstick and its accompanying liner, and now look at them.

"Hey, you remember that time at Star Market?" Mia asked, referencing the airplane hangar of a grocery store down the block from their college dorm.

"Which time? We practically lived there. Not that you ate anything."

"That time we were so stoned and just, like, grabbing fistfuls of shit from the candy bins?"

"'If you're going to steal it, you could at least use a scooper!'" Rachel said, imitating the grocery store clerk who had caught them.

"Damn, it was so bright in there, do you remember? Like the surface of the sun," said Mia. "And she was right, of course. How disgusting of us."

"By the way, are you not eating again?" asked Rachel.

She sighed and gave Mia a look of distress. Sometimes Mia ate like a normal person, and sometimes she didn't; it depended on her mood. As a former chubby person who liked being skinny, it was never not on her mind. She could look at a Twizzler and gain two pounds, and that was just the truth. Or was it? She didn't even know anymore.

"No one likes a fat widow," said Mia.

Rachel groaned.

"It's true!"

"You're an idiot."

"I know." Mia sighed. "I do eat, I swear. I just never sit down."

"Well, you need to eat on your feet or something," said Rachel. She popped the cork expertly, transferring the champagne's exuberant foam to each flute without spilling a drop.

"You look emancipated." Rachel smiled wryly. It was a joke from nine hundred years ago, when they had been college juniors.

"Jesus, Macher, you look emancipated!" Rachel had yelled in a Filene's Basement dressing room. Mia had stood before her naked from the waist up.

"What?"

"Emancipated!"

"You mean emaciated?"

They had laughed because laughter cured everything.

"To your memoir!" said Rachel now. "A forty-three-year-old woman with a memoir. Your mom would be so proud of you, honey."

Mia clinked her flute against Rachel's. "To my mom," she said.

"And to sales!" Rachel said, and raised her flute higher.

"Lord, please!" Mia said, and took a sip. The bubbles popped pleasantly against the roof of her mouth.

Mia's mother had been the most honest person Mia had ever known. This was good and it was bad, but it was mostly bad if you were her daughter.

"It reads like a soap opera, Mia," she had told her sternly, peering over the rims of her glasses the first time fifteen-year-old Mia had asked her to read one of her short stories, a short story Mia was submitting to a city-wide writing contest.

Mia's mother had been in her beloved bed, the blue and white flowers of the pillowcase stark behind her dark head of hair. "You can do better."

She had been right, of course. Mia had begrudgingly rewritten it, and then she had won.

Now her mother's voice lived in Mia's head.

Get to the point!

Too many metaphors! Just say the damn thing is a thing!

Mia's writing was much better for it, she knew that, but in retrospect couldn't her mother have been nicer? Or was she just doing the best she could as a working mother? Nice was a luxury that she had had no time for, literally or figuratively.

"Why you looking so down?" Rachel asked. "No ma'am! This is a triumph! Hustle up." She gestured toward the stairs.

"We're going somewhere?"

"I have some plans for us. Some reservations, if you will."

"Get out," said Mia. "For what?"

"Blowouts and nails, honey. You can't do a book release looking all bedraggled."

"But the dudes, I have to pick them up—"

"Covered," said Rachel. "I texted with Nora. She's picking them up with her girls."

Nora lived next door to Mia, with two daughters the same ages as the dudes.

"Will you be my emergency contact?" Mia had asked her a week after her husband had died as they checked their respective mailboxes.

"Sure," said Nora, although they hadn't really known each other at all. Mia was grateful.

"Wow, thank you," said Mia now. "And Nora."

"We got you," said Rachel. "This is a big night, and you should treat it as such. Now come on, we're going to be late."

The morning after her husband had fallen into a coma, after Mia had spent the night in the hospital sitting next to him in a fog of disbelief, Rachel had been the first call she had made.

"Something bad happened," she had warbled as she stood in her backyard, looking at the lawn he had just mowed. "Something really bad."

"Should I come? I'll come right now," Rachel had said, but Mia had told her to wait. Maybe he would pull out of it. Maybe miracles really did happen?

And then Mia had driven to the hospital, and as she sat next to her husband, freezing in what felt like a meat locker instead of the ICU, Rachel had begun texting George and Chelsea, their numbers still in Rachel's phone from the bachelorette party they had planned for her ten years prior. Unbeknownst to Mia, their chain had gone back and forth, back and forth, until five days later, when Rachel had broken.

"Wheels up," she had texted them from O'Hare. "I'm going in."
Two days later, her husband had died.

ON THE WAY to the salon, as Rachel drove because she knew to take the wheel without asking—she knew that Mia had never liked to drive, but when her husband had died she had no choice but to drive everywhere, all the time—Mia read a new review, this time from *Books Vs. Cats*:

She's giving all of these logistical tips, but what about emotional tips? That's a memoir. This is a biography. One out of five stars.

"One out of five!" Mia snarled, shoving her phone back into her purse.

"Whoa," said Rachel, glancing over at her. "You okay? What happened?"

"Bad review from some asshole." Mia stared out the window: snow and mud, otherwise known as snirt; bare trees; and endless gray. January in Jersey.

"What did she say?" asked Rachel, turning on the left blinker.

Mia's car was a middle-aged Hyundai Santa Fe. From a distance it looked acceptable, but up close you could see the scratches and the dings, the dark green paint faded from the elements because the garage was filled with the detritus of their past and a lifetime supply of paper towels. The interior wasn't any better. The dudes had destroyed the gray leather with their footprints and melted raisins, their spilled milk and vomit.

It was clean, however. Mia made sure of that.

"She called it a biography, not a memoir."

"What did she mean by that?" asked Rachel.

"That the book was all about him and not about me."

"Oh, I see." Rachel pulled into a parking space of the strip mall.

"What?" asked Mia. "What does *I see* mean?"

"Well, she's not wrong," said Rachel carefully. "It is about him. And you with him. Flashbacks and stuff. But the you part is missing a little, don't you think?"

"No," barked Mia, opening her door and climbing out. "And they're not flashbacks, they're interior thoughts. There's a difference. And I wanted to acknowledge his existence. I wanted to help people. I didn't want to put them to sleep."

"Are you saying that you're boring?" asked Rachel as they walked, their breath dissolving into smoke in the frigid air. "Because you're not. You can't be a boring person and handle all this the way you have. You were tough as shit to begin with."

"Oh God, you're not one of those idiots who say, *God doesn't give us anything we can't handle*? Because I will slit your throat if so. That has to be the most patronizing statement of all time."

"Girl, I don't even believe in God, so relax with the throat slitting. I just think you've been able to handle this in a way most people can't, and I know why because I've known you for twenty-something years, but your readers don't know why."

"It's twenty-five," said Mia.

"What's twenty-five?"

"Twenty-five years since we met, not twenty-something."

They stopped just outside the glass front of the salon. There was something about a manicure, and a pedicure immediately afterward, of course, when there was nary a chip or a smudge to be found, when Mia's nail beds and heels were buffed to a shine, that gave Mia a very specifically shallow but no less gratifying feeling of having her shit together even when she didn't. Especially when she didn't.

"Damn, we're old," said Rachel.

Rachel pushed open the door, and a bell heralded their arrival. They were greeted by a chorus of bored hellos from the staff, most of whom didn't look up from their tasks. One of them appeared to be handling a blowtorch.

Mia had come for her first manicure here after her husband had died. No color, no shine. Just clean nail beds. When she had begun to cry looking at her bare ring finger, her tech had handed her a box of tissues and given her a free neck massage instead of asking why. Now, that tech gave Mia a small smile and wave before returning to the feet of a sleeping pregnant woman.

"Manicures and pedicures?" Rachel announced to everyone. "We have appointments?"

"Ah yes," said the owner. "Pick color and then—" She pointed to two empty chairs side by side. From the back, two women emerged, shuffling to their stations.

"Why did you leave yourself so out of your book?" asked Rachel quietly as they faced the wall of nail polish.

"I had this chance to bring him back to life through my words. For readers and for the dudes. And for me." Mia selected a Matisse-colored blue from the wall for her fingers and a barely there nude for her toes from the shelves. "So I took it."

"I love your book," said Rachel as they both climbed into their leather thrones. "But I would have liked more of your story. More about who you are."

Mia submerged her weary feet into the tiny Jacuzzi, shivering with delight as the warm water churned and frothed.

"There is no me," said Mia. "The dudes and I are one. We have to be."

"Do you?"

"Yes!" snapped Mia. Rachel didn't have any kids; she didn't understand. "I don't have the energy to be selfish, anyway."

"Carving out your own identity isn't selfish, Mia. It's healthy. I mean, who are you now? You're a mom, but you can't just be that."

"I'm not! I'm a writer."

"Yes, but not that either. Your kids are your responsibility, your writing is your job—"

"My passion. Writing is my passion," Mia corrected her.

"Fine, but it's still work. What about the rest of you?"

"There is no rest of me," said Mia.

"There needs to be," said Rachel. "Or you're going to run yourself into the ground."

Mia turned on the chair's massage function and closed her eyes. How had she been naive enough to think that reviewers would be kind to her? They were still out for blood, just like they always were, except this was Mia they were criticizing, not a plot or a character she had Frankenstein'd into existence. And now here was Rachel, joining the chorus.

Shit.

"Okay, let's move on," said Rachel. "It's still a beautiful book regardless. And if anyone asks, you just tell them to stay tuned for the next book. You can write about yourself then."

What Rachel didn't understand was that if Mia's memoir

tanked, there would be no next book, not for a very long time, and only if Mia was lucky, which she wasn't.

She had been raised to know that nothing came for free, that everything had to be worked hard for, that *the Machers didn't have luck*. That was what her father had told her when she was small, not for any particular reason that she could remember, but just because he considered it a fact. She had been eating a McDonald's soft-serve ice cream cone at the time, her sneakered feet dangling over the Astroturf of the playground.

Mia had told a therapist about this once. The therapist had said that it was a self-fulfilling prophecy to spout to a five-year-old. That her father had been irresponsible with his words. Mia disagreed. She came from a long line of hardworking masochists. Luck wasn't on her side, but her work spoke for itself, which felt remarkably fulfilling until she compared herself to other writers. Bestselling ones.

And she had worked so hard on the memoir: carving out her morning time every day before her day as a single mom began. Single cooking, single cleaning, single food shopping, single hugging, single crying, single toilet training, single laundering, single walking her elder into his first day of kindergarten.

Of course Mia wasn't in the memoir! Mia had lost herself just trying to stay alive.

"So what part of the book are you going to read from tonight?" Rachel asked as they got their fingernails painted.

Mia stared at the smudge in the nude polish of her big toe. *Don't*, she warned herself, even though she knew that she would.

"The part about getting the phone call from the hospital?

Driving there and thinking all of the things?" Mia answered. "Excuse me, miss? I'm so sorry, but I smooshed my big toe."

"Don't move this time!" the tech yelled at Mia as she removed the polish and started over again.

"I won't, I promise," said Mia.

"I mean it!" she said when she was done.

"She hates me," Mia whispered to Rachel.

"So what?" said Rachel.

"I'm worried that I'm going to cry tonight. At the reading," Mia blurted out as Justin Bieber filtered through tiny speakers nestled into the popcorn ceiling overhead.

She had lost it once on a panel, less than three months after he had died. She had gone because she wanted to prove to herself and the dudes that she could, but she had felt so raw, like her skin had been ripped off under the fluorescent lights of the library.

When the kind moderator had asked her to speak, Mia's eyes had become faucets; there had been nothing she could have done to turn them off. She had remained mute on the panel, studying her shoes instead and praying for it to just be over.

"Sometimes I go on these crying jags out of nowhere—they're horrible. It's like this roller coaster of emotion that I can't get off of, just loop after loop after loop." Mia sniffled, realizing snot was running down her lip, but both hands were occupied.

"Excuse me, can we get some tissues?" Rachel called out. A box was presented, and she used her free hand to dab at Mia's nose.

"Well, this is a new level of intimacy," said Mia, laughing now. "What are you, my mom?"

"Aren't I?" said Rachel, and Mia stopped laughing because what Rachel said was true in a lot of ways.

When Mia had lost her mother at thirty-six, seven years ago now, Rachel had become Mia's life jacket. She had lost her own mother too, at sixteen, and so she knew exactly what to do.

Rachel had always been Mia's wise and practical friend—she had no time for Mia's bullshit with food and about boys, but she had all the time for the mom-size hole in Mia's heart because she had the same hole in her own.

"I know what we can do," Rachel said now. "We can run it like Oprah! I'll ask you the questions, and you'll answer. Like Tom Cruise when he jumped on that couch and showed everybody that he's nuts."

"That image is burned into my retinas," Mia said. "For the rest of my life, I will never be able to unsee it."

"What do you say? Oprah?" asked Rachel.

"I'm not *not* into it," answered Mia.

She thought about all the readings at which she had put the audience to sleep with her monologues. People wanted to be entertained, not lectured.

"No, I'm definitely into it. I can write the questions for you to make it easier," Mia offered, gaining speed. "Are you serious? You'll do it? I would be so grateful—"

"Girl, stop begging. I would do anything for you."

And Mia knew that Rachel would.

CHAPTER 3

"MOM, YOU LOOK PRETTY," SAID HER ELDER when Mia presented herself to the two of them. The dudes were sitting on the couch, nestled into Rachel.

"Beautiful," her younger added, his cherub-cheeked face a light-bulb of pride.

"Aw, thanks, guys," said Mia.

Her husband was so present in these two little humans. The things they said, their mannerisms, the way they looked at her. It made the backbreaking, relentless, *can't you initiate and execute an activity by yourself for once? Just once?* grind worth it.

Most of the time, anyway.

There was a knock at the door, and Mia clomped across the floor in her clogs toward it.

"Hi, Morris," she said.

"Hi, Mia!" Morris stood on the porch in a black T-shirt and basketball shorts. Morris was Mia's former student, from a writing workshop she had taught before everything had gone to shit.

"I'm Red Cross certified," he had informed her solemnly in the community center parking lot where Mia taught, Mia's stomach filled with her younger, who was due the next week. "It would be my honor to babysit your children."

And so she and her husband would book Morris on the too-few occasions they had gone to a movie and dinner or, every once in a blue moon, a house party or birthday celebration where the exhausted parents drank too much and complained about it in the morning.

After her husband had died, Morris had been at the cemetery for the funeral, standing way at the top of the hill, wearing an ill-fitting suit. Mia had seen him from the passenger window of the car on their way into the cemetery.

"Morris, are you nuts! Shorts?" Mia yelled, and pulled him into the house.

"How are you?" she asked him. She hadn't seen him since the funeral. She hadn't gone anywhere without the dudes in three years. Morris had grown up.

"Good," he said. "Back in college part time."

"That's terrific. What are you studying?"

"Botany."

"Oh," said Mia. She had not considered Morris to be a botany kind of person. Computers. IT. Maybe video game coding. But not botany. "How cool."

"Thanks," said Morris.

"So are you still writing?" asked Mia.

Morris was a terrible writer. Mia would not ever tell him this.

"Not really," said Morris.

The dudes sauntered into the room.

"Hey, Morris," they chorused, unbothered by the considerable amount of time that had elapsed.

The four of them walked around the base of the stairwell and into the living room, where Rachel still sat, sipping the last of her champagne.

"Hello!" said Morris.

"I'm Rachel." She stood up and smiled her blinding smile.

"We have to go," said Mia, looking at her watch. As a single parent, she was late to everything, but she didn't want to be late to her own reading.

"Yes!" said Rachel. "Mia Macher can't be late to her own book launch!"

"I have my copy right here," said Morris, pulling it out of his backpack and waving it in front of Mia.

The jacket art was stunning, and Mia was proud of that. Not all of her books could claim that honor. When she had started out as a female author ten years prior, if you were a woman and wrote a book about other women, your book jacket featured the back of a woman's head facing a sunset.

If you were a man and wrote a book attempting the same, your book jacket just had a cool font. Mia found it infuriating.

Why was Mia a *women's fiction* author because she wrote about women but Mr. So-and-So's book about women was deemed literary fiction? Why wasn't there a shelf for men's fiction featuring book jackets covered in giant phalluses and footballs?

"Would you sign it?" asked Morris hopefully.

"Of course," said Mia. "Just let me get a Sharpie."

She ran to the kitchen, where inside a bowl her husband had made with the dudes at a local pottery shop for the last Mother's Day on which he would be alive, and grabbed one.

Mia looked up at the yellow clock tick-tocking on the wall. They were going to be late.

Thanks for the support, Morris! she wrote. *I love you!*

"*I love you*"?

Shit. Well, there was no turning back now. Sharpies were forever.

"Get it together, Mia," she muttered to herself.

She kissed the dudes and grabbed her bag from the couch.

"Bedtime is at eight for the little guy and eight thirty for the big guy," she said as Rachel pulled at her arm.

"Yep," said Morris.

"Their teeth are brushed, just make sure they pee," she said as Rachel closed the door behind her.

"Our Lyft is here," said Rachel, pointing to an electric blue Prius. "Let's go."

CHAPTER 4

"WELCOME, OUR NEIGHBOR MIA MACHER!" Fred Mosley, the bookstore's owner, announced.

Fred was very trim, like horse jockey trim, with a perfectly round and bald head that shone like the sun. He wore a belt around the waistband of his jeans and a blue-and-white-checkered shirt. His basset hound, Bill, lay on the floor below the cash register, looking bored.

A largish crowd of people Mia knew and a few she did not clapped politely. Mia sat, her legs shaking, telling herself to smile.

Out in the audience should be her husband, beaming as he always had. In the front row, taking photos. Reveling in Mia's triumph just as much as, if not more than, she did.

But he was not there.

Her father wasn't either.

"Have your publisher send you down here to the Barnes and Noble," he had told her. He lived outside Atlanta, in the same house Mia had grown up in, with Judy. Judy did not like to fly.

"The one next to the Target," her father had added.

"Yeah, right," Mia had said. "They barely agreed to send me down the street."

She wished her dad was in the audience now, just so she could see his face. She knew his face by heart. Even as it aged and cracked and sprung hair in the most unlikely places, it was still the same face. Their relationship was complicated—Ira seemed to have forgotten Mia's mother ever existed, and Mia resented him for it—but in that moment, her knees shaking slightly onstage as Rachel began, she wished for his face. His black-rimmed glasses and bright blue, deep-set eyes; his unruly eyebrows.

"Hi, everyone, I'd like to introduce myself as the M.C. of tonight's illustrious event. My name is Rachel Martin, and I will be interviewing the heralded Ms. Macher this evening." She paused for effect.

Mia looked at her feet. She had spent forty dollars on the sheer lavender socks that some Instagram influencer with a brain the size of a pea had been wearing with the same yellow clogs Mia already owned. They bunched in pools of sweaty tulle around Mia's ankles, defeated by their lack of purpose.

The crowd laughed for Rachel. Mia recognized her mom friends from the dudes' elementary school sprinkled throughout, perched on black metal folding chairs in varying degrees of athleisure.

"Hi," she mouthed to Emily, who had once provided some emergency wipes on the playground when her younger had pooped behind the swings.

"Hello, Mia," said Rachel, her eyes flashing.

"Hello, Rachel."

Mia could talk about herself if someone was doing the asking, no problem. As a child, the same age as her younger was now, she had spent the time between their lights going out courtesy of her parents and the sleep rolling in courtesy of her subconscious pretending to be interviewed on the *Today* show.

In the dark underneath her Holly Hobbie bedspread, Mia would whisper the questions and then the answers, playing the roles of both Bryant Gumbel and herself. She was a movie star on-air to promote her latest film; she was a badass executive on Wall Street; she was a model. She was an author.

Oh, yes, I did all my own stunts, Mia would whisper to her Cabbage Patch doll, Penelope Amherst, envisioning a giant purple belt cinched around her tiny fantasy waist.

"Mia, tell us what your memoir is about," said Rachel now.

"Well," said Mia. "My husband died, very unexpectedly, two years and nine months ago." The audience murmured and shifted in their seats.

Don't feel sorry for me, thought Mia. *Yeah, it sucks. Feel sorry for me,* she thought next.

"So the book is about that moment and my journey since, as a single mom of two young boys. They were only five and newly two when he died."

As she explained this, a very distinct memory surfaced of her younger, blowing out a candle in a birthday donut at the dining room table, his father's precarious position in a hospital bed twenty miles away unbeknownst to him because he was just two. Two.

"It's one of the saddest stories I've ever heard," said Rachel, "except of course I've been watching you live it."

"It's interesting you put it that way," said Mia. "Because even still sometimes I'm unable to process the fact that the sad cable movie of the week is about me."

"Oh, honey, give yourself a little bit more credit," said Rachel. "You're definitely HBO material." Mia smiled.

"When you talk about your journey, what exactly do you mean?" Rachel continued.

"Well, my life was obliterated when he died," Mia answered. "Obviously it wasn't going to look anything like I thought it would. My memoir is about what that felt like. What it still feels like."

"Life as a single mother," said Rachel.

"Yes," said Mia.

"A widow," said Rachel.

"Yes."

"The sole earner in your household."

"Okay, now you're just stressing me out," said Mia.

A few members of the audience laughed nervously; the discomfort in the room was palpable.

"So why did you decide to write a memoir about such a painful time in your life? Wasn't living it hard enough?"

"Well, writing is how I process things. I've always done that, since I was a little girl. I always loved to read, and I always loved to write. I started journaling when I was eight years old. My parents really encouraged it."

"What sorts of things did you write about?" asked Rachel.

Mia thought back. Her journals had been about two things during her entire journaling career: food and boys. With the arrival of her husband, she hadn't seemed to need it any longer. When she was missing her mom, she told him or wove her into a character she was creating, and that felt just as good. Or did it? Mia wasn't sure.

"The usual," said Mia finally. "I stopped journaling when I met my husband, though."

"Why?" asked Rachel.

"I think I maybe got lost in him a little bit, the way we all do when we fall in love. I was so . . ." She searched for a word that was a little more sophisticated than the one that blinked in her subconscious like a pink neon sign but couldn't find one. "Happy," she finished.

"So writing is more of an outlet for you when you're unhappy?" asked Rachel.

"I guess so," said Mia. "And lord knows I was unhappy when I wrote this memoir. Just this crushing sadness—the sadness of missing him for my own but really more for the dudes' sake, along with the sadness of realizing that control is just an illusion, you know? The universe doesn't give a fuck about your plans, no matter how many spreadsheets you make."

Rachel widened her eyes at Mia, and Mia understood that through this gesture she was asking her if she was okay to keep going, because Mia's voice had started to tremble and the audience was shifting forward and back and side to side in their chairs, trying to un-notice what they had noticed.

If grief made people uncomfortable just hearing her speak

about it, how in the world could she expect people to want to pay money to read about it?

Shit.

"I'M ROSE," SAID a woman in the book-signing line as Mia took an enormous gulp of warm white wine from her clear plastic cup. "You're amazing," she told Mia.

"I'm not," said Mia.

"No, you are," she insisted. "Losing a husband, writing a book, taking care of two little kids. I can't imagine."

A pet peeve of Mia's was when people told her they "couldn't imagine." Actually, they could imagine her situation with minimal effort. Mia knew that they were just trying to be kind, but she wished they would just say that.

"Well, thank you," said Mia instead. "How do you spell your name?"

Outside in the cold air, after the last book had been signed and Mia had asked Fred if she could help clean up but had been shooed outside instead, she ducked into the alley and lit a victory cigarette.

She had done it: her first book without him.

Her husband had been there for all her book launches. She could see him lying on the couch, his long frame and giant, black-socked feet dangling off its edge, his head against a pillow, her last book on his baby blue fleece-covered chest. They used to call that fleece "the towel," and while Mia was fairly certain a previous girlfriend of his had named it that, it was the perfect description, and so Mia had allowed it to stay.

"Hey, Mia, this is really good!" he had called to her in the other room, and her heart had swelled.

Now her heart ached not only with the missing of him, it ached with the missing of her with him. They had only been together for ten years, a drop in the bucket in the grand scheme of things, if Mia was lucky enough to live for eighty-four or so, but it had been the happiest ten years of her life.

Mia wanted to be that happy again, but she didn't see how it was possible. There was a blessed naïveté at the root of it that she could never access again. Not even a little bit. She ground out her cigarette into the ground and ripped off her stupid socks.

"Rachel?" she called into the night, and left the alley behind.

"That was so much fun," said Rachel, plunging a French fry into a pool of ketchup. "We were great up there."

"We were," said Mia. She took a fry for herself. She hadn't eaten dinner, so it was okay.

God, she was so boring. Forty-three years old and still giving herself permission to eat.

"So why do you look so sad?" Rachel asked. She sat back against the maroon leather of the booth and folded her arms across her chest. "You must be missing him, huh?"

"I am," said Mia. "He should be here."

"He should," agreed Rachel. "This world is bullshit. All of these assholes live forever, and the good ones have to die."

"That's certainly what it seems like," said Mia. "You know what I realized up on that stage, though?"

"What?"

"This book is doomed."

"Why?"

"Nobody wants to read about death right now. The world is garbage with this fucked-up government. I should have made it funny or something," said Mia, and then she sighed a deep, sad sigh.

"Yeah, I miss the funny Mia. Hashtag funny widow?" Rachel said, making a joke.

"Hashtag fun widow," said Mia, shaping it more to her liking. "I should have posted photos from the funeral home, picking out coffins."

"That's dark," said Rachel through her laughter.

"Hashtag fun widow, me crying in the shower," Mia continued. "Hashtag fun widow, me getting my car serviced. Damnit, I should have had my head in the game, been marketing this from the get-go." She was laughing now too. It was just all too goddamn sad.

"I'm not fun anymore," said Mia, once she'd composed herself.

"I wouldn't call you a barrel of laughs," said Rachel.

"Thanks."

Would she ever have fun again? Mia wondered. Now that she knew what she knew—that death wasn't on a schedule, that she could have the wind knocked out of her literally or figuratively or both at any time—she couldn't not know it. Exuberance had never been Mia's strong suit, but it felt impossible now.

"You'll be back, I know you will," Rachel told her. "Fun will be different, but everything else is different, so why not? Remember when I went to London, for semester abroad?" She leaned forward and put both elbows on the table.

A waitress approaching turned on her white-sneakered heel at the sight of them tête-à-têting, emitting a squeak in her wake as she headed to another booth instead.

"Of course—you deserted me, and I had to live with some wackjob girl from Connecticut who pretended to be British."

"I would wait by the mailbox for your letters," said Rachel, ignoring Mia's complaints. "Your antics with that dude, what was his name?"

"I.T.," said Mia, remembering.

Mia had named him such because he was in her computer class. None of the boys they dated or obsessed over in college had real names. Rachel had dated a guy they called "The Hulk" for two years because of his unfortunate pallor.

"My memoir wasn't funny," said Mia.

"There were parts that were," said Rachel. "That was progress enough for me. Two years ago I was mailing you Valium because you couldn't get out of bed, for God's sake. You've come a long way."

"But there's still so far to go," whined Mia. "But I'm willing, I guess. For the dudes."

"The dudes, yes," said Rachel, "but the universe too."

"What are you talking about?"

"Ira's dream," said Rachel.

"Oh," said Mia.

Ira had called Mia breathless the morning after her husband had died and told her that he had seen her husband in a dream, that he had told Ira that *Barbara says hello*. Barbara was Mia's mother.

A born cynic, there was no way Ira would have lied about the dream, although Mia had asked him anyway. It had seemed too beautiful to be real.

"Why would I lie at seven in the morning?" asked Ira, as though lying in the afternoon was more likely.

It had been the most reassuring thing, much less dream, that Mia had ever heard. Her husband's soul hurtling through space and time to relay her mother's message to her grieving father. The soul did go on. Magic was real. There was a point to life, after all.

"Why didn't you put that in the memoir?" Rachel asked.

"I dunno, it felt too loosey-goosey," said Mia. "I didn't want anyone to take it away from me. I have trouble believing it as it is."

"How are you and Mitch?" Mia asked. If she didn't, Rachel would trick her into talking about herself forever. Mitch was Rachel's husband. He had been out of work for eighteen months—seventeen too long, according to Rachel.

"There's not much to say. He's still sitting on his ass all day, except when he has the audacity to go to yoga. Do you know that motherfucker still calls me at work every day to ask what we're doing for dinner? I don't know, you tell me, Mitch! Damn."

"Oh no," said Mia. She liked Mitch. He was a good man, and Flannery O'Connor had taught her that those were hard to find.

"What's up with your book tour?" asked Rachel, swinging the pendulum back to Mia.

"This is it."

"Get out. Wait, what? You've written five books!"

"My publisher would barely pay for the cheese cubes tonight, there's no fucking way they're flying me all over the country for a memoir that's not a memoir. And lord knows I can't afford it."

"You write it off!"

"Even then, Rachel."

"So ask George to help out! Isn't her husband a millionaire? I bet he has miles for days. Actually I bet between the three of us we could sponsor you no sweat."

"Sponsor me? What am I, entering a read-a-thon? I can't accept that," said Mia. "It's too generous. And anyway, I don't know if Chelsea and George would be up for it."

"What do you mean?" asked Rachel. "Why wouldn't they be up for it?"

"Well, George is obviously going through something. She posts these long-winded and poorly written diatribes on Instagram about nothing—"

"Yeah, I've seen those," said Rachel, wincing.

"And Chelsea's kid is super high maintenance."

"Sounds like they need you."

"Need me? Who needs a houseguest when they're swirling down the drain?"

"You did."

"Oh," said Mia. "You're right. That's when I needed you most."

"So what's the problem?" asked Rachel. "I'll send them a group text."

"But I can't afford the tickets," said Mia.

Her father had told her never to take help from anyone because the other person always expected something in return, but then again her father had never had friends. Her mother had been his life.

"But we can," said Rachel. "And there are no strings. Don't even start with that."

"Well," said Mia, reconsidering. "Maybe that could work. I could write an email for you guys to send to your local bookstore, asking for readings."

She did want to get the hell out of Dodge, if only so that she didn't have to make or clean up after anyone's meals for a few days. If only because she could go for a walk without a giant backpack filled with water bottles and Band-Aids and wipes and snacks and jackets and tiny plastic superheroes strapped to her shoulders. Just to walk down a street with nothing in her hands but a paper coffee cup from an overpriced café. That was living.

"Now you're talking," said Rachel. She motioned to the waitress.

"We'll both have another drink," she said. "So when can we make the tour happen? George is still in San Francisco, right? It's a lot to travel to San Francisco, Chicago, and then Atlanta in one go."

Rachel was a follow-througher, the best kind of friend.

"Yeah, but I would need one go because of the dudes. I can't be coming and going willy-nilly. No babysitter would be down with that. Let's see." Mia paused to picture the flight map in her head. "I guess a week would be good? One week. God, what am I thinking, I can't be away from them for one week! I can't even take out the garbage without one of them running out of the house looking for me."

"You can. They're good dudes. You tell them you're going on a book tour to make money to send them to college. This is your job. Period. End of story."

Rachel slid out of her side of the booth and sat next to Mia.

"You're always so warm," said Mia quietly.

"It's because I eat," said Rachel. "My blood circulates. You should try it sometime."

"I'm just, I think I need to find a new career," said Mia, ignoring her. "This writing thing, it's selfish. I barely pay the mortgage, and I've been at this thing for ten years. Real money? Savings? Stability? I have none of that."

"What do you have?" asked Rachel.

"A job that I love," said Mia.

"Exactly. That's exactly right. How many people do you know who love what they do?"

"I—"

"How many people do you know who can use their passion to inspire other people's passion? Selfish, my ass. You articulate emotions that people don't even know they have. Your work is art, and art is important."

"That's all very kind of you to say," said Mia, "and I appreciate it, but at what cost? At this rate, I can't send my kids to college. I can barely send them to day camp."

"Money isn't going to make you happy, Mia. Your dudes are happy. Do you know how extraordinary that is? They lost their father, and still they are happy. That's because of you."

Mia blew her nose loudly into the black cloth napkin on the table.

"Well, that's just gross," said Rachel.

"Sorry."

"Mia. Listen to me." Rachel reached out and turned Mia's face toward hers, so they were looking directly into each other's eyes. "You gotta get back to yourself for a minute." Her hand gripped Mia's chin tightly.

"You're hurting me." Rachel loosened her fingers, and Mia exhaled. "But I can never pay you back," she told her.

"We don't give a shit about getting paid back. Your art is the currency."

"But it's not right, to depend on you like this."

"You are the most independent, take-care-of-business human I know. You're not depending on anybody but you. Nobody works harder than you. Everybody knows that."

"My dad doesn't know that," said Mia.

"Oh, fuck your dad. He said something stupid because he's a caveman."

It had been two months after her husband had died when he had said it. Mia had flown with the dudes down to Atlanta to visit him and Judy in the scorching August sun because they had booked it before her husband had died, and since it had always been their intention to go, they were going regardless. It had still felt so surreal then to Mia—her husband wasn't really dead; he was going to meet them at the airport, that was all.

The day Ira had said it, Mia had been in a medicated fog because it hurt too much just to breathe. Ira had been sitting behind her on the couch; the U.S. Open had been on the television because the television was never not on, not ever, in his house.

"You know, you gotta stop feeling sorry for yourself," he had told her over the *pock-pock* of the bouncing ball.

"What?" Mia had asked incredulously, her toes already curled. Her father had always been like this, he had always had the emotional intelligence of a fruit fly, but this. This was a new low.

"It's enough already. You gotta get on with your life. You gotta make a living for these boys."

"It hasn't even been three months!" Mia had snarled, turning around and facing him on all fours like a Doberman pinscher.

"I see your friends giving you presents and taking you places. You gotta cut that out," he barreled on, completely unbothered by Mia's mounting hysteria. "There is no free lunch. They're gonna come collect."

And then Mia had slapped him across the face and walked out of the house. She had had to return twenty minutes later, naturally, since she had no shoes on, but she and her father had not spoken of it again. He was who he was, she knew that, but not about this. Not on her watch.

"I really believe in you," said Rachel now. "You're the girl who walked back and forth from campus every goddamn day for four years, in rain, sleet, and snow, even though there was a T running right beside you. You needed the exercise, you wanted the fresh air, you said, and so you got it. You don't even see obstacles. You never have.

"Now listen to me: you're going to hit the big time with some book someday, because you have the talent and you have the motherfucking drive. And when you do, you'll take us out on your yacht."

My yacht. That would be nice.

"What do I do with the dudes for a week if I go on this book tour?" asked Mia.

"What about Nora? Can't she and her husband watch them? They all go to the same school, don't they? Shit, they could even sleep in their own beds since they're right next door."

"They're kids, Rachel, not cats. No, I can't ask a mother of two to watch two more for a whole week, that's insane."

"What about the husband?"

"What about him?"

"Oh, okay," said Rachel. "Well, what about your dad and Judy, then?" The waitress plunked down two more martinis at their table and continued on her way, a plate of nachos balanced on her forearm.

"One more of these and I'll be cross-eyed," said Mia.

"That's the plan."

"And no way in hell am I asking my dad and Judy to come squat in my house for a week, to answer your question. You know how I feel about Judy."

Judy had married Mia's father with no regard for Mia. She was the kind of person who never asked Mia how she was; the kind of person who left her dirty dishes in the sink. Judy was not her mother.

"Fine, then what about just your dad? If he has Nora on call and a freezer full of pizzas, what's the problem?"

Ira had been the most involved father of all of Mia's friends, who barely saw their fathers other than on the weekends when football wasn't on. Ira had taught her to read, how to ride a bike, how to write an essay. When she was eighteen and leaving for college, he had wordlessly driven into a CVS parking lot, left her in the car, and returned with a twelve-pack of condoms.

"You're going to need these," he had said, and thrown them into her virgin lap, the plastic sticking to her bare legs. He had been right.

He had been a great father, the best Mia had ever known until she had seen her husband father their dudes. But she was so mad at her father now. Less than two years after her mother had died, after forty-four years of their marriage, Ira had married someone new.

He was a cliché. The worst thing to be.

But he was also a terrific grandfather: playing catch, asking questions, wrestling with the dudes when his seventy-three-year-old body was up for it. And the dudes needed more male influence in their lives. Just last week her elder had gotten dirt on his hands and held them up to Mia as though they were on fire.

"Fine, I'll ask him," said Mia. "But no Judy."

"Fuck Judy," said Rachel.

CHAPTER 5

Mia climbed up the stairs, coffee in hand. She had just walked the dudes to school in the arctic air, two Labrador puppies, pawing and nipping at each other incessantly until they entered the building, leaving glorious quiet in their wake.

She opened the blinds to the windows over her desk and sat down, emitting a quiet sigh about the task that was at hand. Self-promotion. Branding. Going viral, which always sounded vaguely STDish to Mia.

God, she hated it. That said, if you were a mid-list author like Mia was, meaning that your books sold but they didn't *really* sell, it was a necessary evil. There was always the hope that somehow, by some six-degrees-of-separation way, your post would make it onto some celebrity's assistant's feed and magically scratch whatever book to film itch they needed scratching at that precise moment.

Right place, right Twitter feed, and wham! Mia knew that the odds of this happening were slim to none, but she had seen it happen to other authors, and so she had to try.

"Hashtag fun widow," she said out loud to no one, and then she laughed. It was all so ridiculous. She didn't have it in her.

Mia got up, coffee still in hand, and walked over to her bathroom, the one that she and her husband had sworn would be the first thing they'd renovate once they actually had money.

She pulled her hair back with a cheetah-spotted headband the size of a welder's helmet and looked at her scrubbed face, her tired eyes, her giant eyebrows, and laughed at her reflection. No way she was throwing her middle-aged face into the social media ring. It wasn't that she didn't like her face—Mia finally did at forty-three—but what did it have to do with her writing? Zero.

What she would be doing instead was plotting out her book tour, Mia decided as she turned out the bathroom light and made a beeline for her desk. She would tackle its logistics with an outline.

Outlines were the way she wrote books, but they were also the way she did everything else too. Mia could follow any plan that involved Roman numerals. She was especially smug about her grocery list. Sure, it was the produce section of ShopRite, but it was also her literal entry point. Mia strategized accordingly:

I. *Meat*
II. *Vegetables*
III. *Fruit*
IV. *Dairy*
V. *Miscellaneous*

She pushed her laptop back to the edge of her desk now, just beneath the windowsill, and opened up a red college-ruled notebook. Mia had always just had two notebooks—a yellow one for business and a purple one for pleasure—but she had recently purchased a red one for the situations in which business actually was pleasure, because she wanted to manifest that destiny and also because she loved notebooks almost as much as she loved outlines.

I. THE BOOK TOUR: 3/1–3/5/20, she wrote on its first page.
    A. San Francisco with George
    B. Chicago with Rachel
    C. Atlanta with Chelsea

No, that wouldn't do, Mia thought, and ripped out the page to start over.

I. THE BOOK TOUR: 3/1–3/5/20
    A. San Francisco with George
      1. Reading Sunday, 3/1
      2. Leave Monday, 3/2
    B. Chicago with Rachel
      1. Reading Tuesday, 3/3
      2. Leave Wednesday, 3/4
    C. Atlanta with Chelsea. Judy?
      1. Reading Wednesday, 3/4
      2. Return home Thursday, 3/5

Mia sat back, cracking her spine against the frame of her chair. It had not escaped her that outlines were meaningless big picture because of course no one had any control at all ultimately; she knew that firsthand. But that was exactly the point.

Her three closest friends, Mia thought, examining the mostly blank piece of college-ruled notebook paper. They did for Mia, again and again, but what had she done for them? Nothing since her husband had died, nothing in two and a half years. That was a lot of nothing.

They had upended their lives for her. They visited; they drove the dudes to every adventure park hellscape in a hundred-mile radius and fed them to boot. Presents would arrive in the mail out of nowhere at exactly the right time, filled with perfumed lotion and face masks, a Dolly Parton mug, LEGO sets for the dudes so she could at least shave her legs in peace.

What could Mia offer, to ease her own conscience at the very least? She supposed she could bring them an overpriced graphic T-shirt, but really, who needed another one of those? Mia could have a whole conversation with her closet if she wanted to.

Maybe she could help them? Mia shifted in her seat; she grabbed her pencil. Mia's advice from the other side of marriage was good for something, wasn't it? That was what her book was about, for God's sake. She ripped out the page and crumpled it neatly into a ball before tossing it into the wicker bin at her feet.

   I. THE BOOK TOUR: 3/1–3/5/20
      A. San Francisco with George
         1. Reading Sunday, 3/1
         2. Instagram intervention

George posted to Instagram incessantly. There was not a trip, a purchase, a wrinkle, a juice cleanse, a milestone that went undocumented. It hadn't always been that way, but since her only job now seemed to be as her plastic surgeon husband's walking billboard, not a day went by without an update on nothing. George looked good—she'd been botoxed and lifted and vacuumed in all the right places—but Mia worried about her.

If Mia was overposting, she was in the dark place.

I'm still here, but I'm all screwed up. Do you see me? she was asking, but no one ever did. Not really.

George, birth name Georgia, came from money, and so did her suitors. A photograph of six-year-old George in a smocked cotton dress on the steps of her family's beach house in Nantucket, her two front teeth missing and a giant red bow atop her freckled head, had stood on her bedside table when she and Mia had shared an apartment, and Mia always found herself staring at it when she was stoned, marveling at a childhood that was nothing like her own.

Mia and George had nothing in common—they had been set up as roommates by friends of friends—and yet somehow they had gotten each other right off the bat in the way that fated friends do. Their friendship was not one for the bars or clubs they frequented on different sides of town with different sets of people; it was for their living room, which spilled into George's room, which spilled into Mia's room, which spilled right into the drain in the middle of their mildewed bathroom floor.

Some people didn't want to be seen, and there was a very good chance that George was one of them, but Mia had to try.

> *3. Leave Monday, 3/2*
> *B. Chicago with Rachel*
> *   1. Reading Tuesday, 3/3*
> *   2. Dog*
> *   3. Or cat*

Mia loved Mitch and Mia loved Rachel, and Mia loved Mitch and Rachel together. Their problems were not systemic. Mia reasoned they were a consequence of Mitch's unemployment. They needed a purpose. Enter a dog. Or a cat. Did they have hairless dogs? Mia wondered, and made a note.

> *4. Leave Wednesday, 3/4*
> *C. Atlanta with Chelsea*
> *   1. Reading Wednesday, 3/4*
> *   2. Let Monica help*

Mia was a Macher and Chelsea was a Lyon, and so they had met in the recess line on the first day of third grade.

I like your T-shirt, Mia had told Chelsea, because she did. She burned with longing for an Esprit T-shirt too, but her mother would never pay retail, not ever. Chelsea was as foreign to Mia as an exchange student from Mars: blonde, skinny, and Baptist, with a mother who put Little Debbies in her lunch. It had been love at first sight.

They had done everything together: bike rides to the Circle K for Now and Laters and Coke slushies; toaster waffles on TV trays for their six hundred viewings of *Grease;* fantasizing about the popular boys who never looked at them. Well, Mia had been fantasizing.

"Mia, I have something to tell you," Chelsea had declared on the other end of her dorm room phone in Ohio, after they had been at college for six weeks.

Now Chelsea was married to Monica. They had a son named River. River was a pain in the ass.

He had been born a pain in the ass and was now formally diagnosed as one, but his medicine was forever being tweaked and tailored to his growth and thus was useless as far as Mia could tell. She felt badly about thinking so poorly of her best friend's son, but she had never expressed her distaste out loud. Chelsea worked so hard to keep him afloat, Mia would never.

Monica was forever on the sidelines, and not of her own accord, Mia suspected.

"It's easier if I just do it," Chelsea said whenever Mia questioned her load. That wasn't true. It wasn't actually easier if one partner did everything, and Mia was proof.

D. Judy
1. arghhhhhhhhhhhhhhhhhhhhhh

Judy had married Mia's father on a beach in Hawaii with a lei of orchids draped around her neck. Fuck Judy.

Fuck Judy because Mia hadn't even known about Hawaii until after the fact, when Ira had casually mentioned it over the phone.

Fuck Judy because her father went on fishing trips with her sons.

Fuck Judy because when Mia's husband had died, she had sent her a card in the mail. *I'm Sorry for Your Loss,* it had read in silver cursive across its front, with Judy's signature inside. *Judy Crenshaw,* as if there were any other Judys.

Mia threw her pencil onto the desk. She knew that her father was happy, she knew that that was all that mattered, she knew she was behaving like an asshole, but she just couldn't get on board with Judy.

Her father had understood Mia's hurt initially, but he was not known for his patience. Now, four years later, he *had had it with Mia's bullshit.* Sometimes Mia was too, to be honest, but she had come too far to turn back.

If you're going to do it, do it right, Ira had told her over and over as a kid. And so here she was, seeing it through. Doing it right. Hating Judy until the bitter end.

That said, Mia knew it would be unconscionable for her to not tell Judy she was coming. Her mother had raised her better than that, irony withstanding.

Mia would email Judy. Maybe lunch? Lunch was benign.

2. Return home Thursday, 3/5
II. DAD, she wrote next.

Could she really expect him to keep the dudes alive for six days? He couldn't even boil water without written instructions.

Mia grabbed her phone.

"Hello," said Ira, mid-chew.

"What are you eating?" she asked him.

"A Twizzler." It was 8:20 A.M.

"Hey, Dad?" asked Mia.

"Yes, my Mia," he replied, and Mia smiled at the phone. She hadn't been very nice to her father since Judy, but he loved her still. Wasn't that something? She knew that it was.

"What's doing?" he asked next. "Everything okay?"

"Oh yeah, we're fine."

"How are the dudes?" he asked.

"Good. Cute as ever. How are you?"

"I woke up today, you know, so I can't complain," he answered.

"So, Dad, listen," said Mia. "Could you watch the dudes for six days in March? I have the opportunity to go on a book tour."

She felt shame as the words came out of her mouth and then anger at the shame. This was her job. She was working. Wasn't that what grandparents were for? Favors? But was it Ira who made her feel this shame and anger or Mia who made herself feel it? At what point did you stop blaming your parents for who you were?

"Why not?" he asked.

She heard him pull a chair across the floor and knew he was sitting by the back window, peering through the blinds like he always did when he spoke on the phone.

"Are you sure? They're so much work."

"I know. I can do it."

"You can?"

"Sure I can. I raised you, didn't I? When do you want us?"

"No," said Mia. "Dad, no Judy. Just you."

"Mia. Come on now, don't be ridiculous. Judy is wonderful with them."

"I don't care if she's Mother Teresa. She's not their grandmother, and I don't want her to come."

The truth was that Judy was fine with the dudes. They liked her, even, but they liked everybody. Plus, Judy wasn't a dummy—she showed up with gifts.

"Excuse me, she's the only grandmother they've ever known. You're being very fresh, Mia, and I don't appreciate it. It's been eight years since your mother died, when are you going to get over this?"

"Seven years! Not eight. And forget it," said Mia. "Forget I even asked. I'll think of someone else."

"Now wait a minute, Mia Rose, just wait. You're going to leave them with a stranger because I so much as suggest that I might want to bring my wife? She would be a great help. I'm not young anymore, you know."

"Just forget it, Dad. Seriously."

"But why can't she come?" he asked. "Give me a good reason other than your own absurdity?"

"That's the only reason you need. They're my kids, and I get to decide who they spend time with."

"Yeah, good luck with that when they're teenagers."

"Bye, Dad."

She was on fire, so hot with anger that she pulled her shirt off right there at the desk and sat in her bra.

So what was she going to do now? Ask George, Rachel, and Chelsea to fly in and take shifts when she wasn't visiting them? That was insane. Why, just once, couldn't her father be a yes-guy?

All her life, he had been a no-guy.

"Dad, can I ride my bike to Mandy's?"

"No, her parents park their cars in the yard, you're not going over there."

"Dad, can I have fifty dollars?"

"You're out of your mind if you think I'm going to pay for you to be a horse's ass."

Mia's mascot had been a mustang at the time. It was all she had ever wanted to be.

Her phone rang.

"What?" Mia answered.

"Oh for Christ's sake, I'll do it," said her dad. "Give me the dates."

CHAPTER 6

"WHAT HANDSOME FELLOWS YOU ARE," IRA told the dudes. Their perfectly round faces beamed up at him.

"These are very good-looking young men," he told Mia.

"Thanks, Dad," said Mia.

Throughout her childhood, Ira had told Mia that she was *pretty as a picture and sharp as a whip,* and she remembered the exact cadence of his voice even now. It was amazing what the brain held on to.

"Can I get you anything?" she asked him now.

The tips of his ears were bright red still, from standing outside Newark Airport and shouting, "Terminal C! C!" into his phone repeatedly at Mia, even though he was standing outside Terminal B.

"You got a bubbly water? That orange kind?"

"We do!" her younger answered triumphantly, and ran to the refrigerator to retrieve it.

"Well, you look beautiful too," her father told her. "Like a movie star."

"Dad!"

"You do." He opened his seltzer with trembling hands.

"What's with your hands?" she asked him.

"The doctor says it's nothing to worry about. My mother had it too."

"Nothing to worry about? You're spilling seltzer all over the counter. How can it be nothing?"

"I need to call Judy, tell her that I made it," said Ira. "You know, your behavior is disgraceful. Judy has never, and I mean never, been anything but gracious to you."

"Does 'gracious' mean 'politely ignore'?"

"That's a lie," said her father.

"It's not."

Now that Mia was a widow herself, she was completely dumbfounded by her father's behavior. Who got married again to a lady they met in the fish aisle of Petco, just two years later? It was disrespectful. Her poor mother.

"So, Dad," Mia said. "I printed up a schedule for you. Do you want to go over it?"

"A schedule? For what?"

"The dudes."

"What are they, infants? They're in their mid-twenties at this point and you're making me a schedule."

"Dad, they're eight and five. They have school. They have basketball practice."

"No basketball practice. They'll be at Camp Ira!" he proclaimed, winking at Mia.

Every summer, for twelve years of Mia's childhood, her father had run Camp Ira, population: two: Ira and Mia. As a high school math teacher, he had had the summers off, and so while her friends were lying on the couch and watching *Saved by the Bell* in their bathing suits, Mia had been writing book reports, finding square roots, and running the high school track with him at high noon, her sweat dripping into the red clay beneath her feet.

The summer before her sophomore year of high school had been her last at Camp Ira, when he had flunked her for a plagiarized essay on Napoleon. She had pretended not to care, but she didn't like to disappoint her father. Not then and not now.

"Yeah, good luck with that," said Mia. "The dudes would never. I have to bribe them to even walk around the block."

"Watch me," said Ira. "Hey, dudes, you ready for Camp Ira?" he yelled toward the adjoining room in which they sat, mesmerized by the glow of their iPads.

"What?" her elder yelled back.

"See?" said Ira. "They're thrilled. Okay, so slide it over," he said, motioning to the piece of paper Mia held in her hand.

"I made a lasagna, it's in the fridge. You can feed them that for dinner the first two nights," she read. "And then—"

"No lasagna," said Ira. "Fruit surprise."

"Dad," said Mia. "Lasagna. And for the other two nights I made this chicken thing, it's right here." She opened the fridge and pointed to it. "And then I thought one night you could go out?"

"Fruit surprise," said her father again.

When Mia's mother, a social worker, had traveled to the occasional work conference, Mia's father had manned the decks. There were two dinners in his repertoire: boxed macaroni and cheese and fruit surprise, which meant *Surprise! It's cut-up fruit and cereal for dinner.*

Mia's mother had handled the cooking and the cleaning and the laundry, and Ira had handled the schooling and the rearing, with very few overlaps. That was how their family had worked.

"I made their lunches for school and labeled them with the days of the week," Mia continued. "All you have to do is put them in their lunch boxes every morning. And don't forget their waters."

"God, you and their waters. They can't go next door without a gallon in hand. It's absurd.

"Where are you going on this book tour?" Ira asked her, even though she had emailed and texted him her exact itinerary. Twice.

"I'm giving readings in San Francisco, Chicago, and Atlanta," recited Mia. "I had to hustle to even get them, of course, but Rachel, George, and Chelsea helped a lot."

"Nice girls," said Ira. "Is George still married to that dud?"

"Dad," said Mia.

"Well, is she?"

"Yes." George's husband, Todd, was self-involved and dumb but thought he was generous and smart. Mia hated him.

"And what about that Rachel? Is she still with the Jewish guy? Does he have a job yet?"

"He's always had a job, Dad. He's a humor writer."

"But how does he make any money?"

"I don't know! Jesus, Dad, I have enough to worry about."

"And what about Chelsea? She still keeping the weight off?"

When Mia had met Chelsea in the third grade, they hadn't yet known that being chubby was a bad thing to be. Madonna's "La Isla Bonita" was on repeat in Chelsea's front—not the back but the front—yard every day as they gyrated in charm necklaces and bathing suits.

Then middle school had happened and Chelsea had locked herself in her bedroom one summer, only to emerge three months later sixty pounds thinner. It didn't matter what else Chelsea achieved in her life—this was her peak moment, according to Ira.

"She had a goal and she achieved it," Ira said now, shaking his head in wonder. It was what he always said.

"Dad, she practically starved herself to death," said Mia.

"Well? It worked, what can I tell you?" He took a sip of his seltzer. "So what's the plan? To sell copies? People actually come to these things?"

"Sometimes," said Mia.

"Wow, big time!" said Ira.

"I don't know about that," said Mia. "I'm also hoping to get some sort of clarity for myself, on who I was and who I am now and how to get back there while still moving forward—"

"What?" asked Ira. "Oh for God's sake, no more of this hooey New Age shit, please. Who you were and you are, give me a break. You're a writer. You were always a writer. Everything else in your life has changed, but that remains the same. What you need to do is start dating again. The dudes need a father, and you need a friend."

"I have lots of friends!" Mia yelled.

"Sex is important, Mia," said Ira.

"Dad, gross."

"What? It is. Keeps you young."

"Ugh, I have no interest. Men need sex more than women do anyway," said Mia. "Lord knows you did."

"Your mother wanted me to meet someone new. She told me that on her deathbed."

"She did not," argued Mia.

"She did! Swear to God."

"Well, she didn't mean it."

"Of course she meant it. When did your mother ever say anything she didn't mean?"

"Fair," said Mia.

"Listen, have a good time on your trip. I'll take care of the dudes; you don't have to worry about them. Sell some books." He patted her back, the warmth of his hand as familiar as her own.

"Okay," she replied. "I will."

CHAPTER 7

MIA SQUINTED AS SHE ROLLED HER SUITCASE toward the airport monitor, feeling warm in her sweater. She stopped to pull it over her head, revealing a very white slice of belly.

She had just experienced the most relaxing six hours and twenty-eight minutes of her life on a plane, after taking a Klonopin to soothe her jangling nerves, all of which had been standing on end by the time she had made it to Newark in the pitch-black hour of four thirty A.M. It was the first time Mia had left the dudes since their father had left for work one morning and never came back.

It had not been an easy departure. They had asked her if she was going to die as she had put them to bed the night before. She still bathed them. She knew they were too old for that and that she was doing their future selves no favors, but she also knew that bath time would soon officially be over and that she would miss it very much. There was little in her life better than snuggling into the bathed backs of her lavender-scented dudes as they drifted to sleep.

"Are you going to die?" her elder had asked her.

"Like on this trip?"

"Yes," her younger solemnly chimed in.

"I really don't think so," she had told them. "I just have a hard time believing that the universe would do that to us too. It would be incredibly cruel."

"What's 'cruel'?" her younger had asked.

"Mean," Mia replied. "I can't tell you that I'm absolutely, definitely, no way going to die on this trip because we already know that that's not how it works, right? We don't know when death is going to come for us, so all we can do is be our best."

"Do your best and fuck the rest!" her younger said quietly, blue eyes sparkling at the forbidden pleasure of that word rolling off his tongue.

That was the energy Mia had carried them to bed on, but after they had fallen asleep and she could finally sit down, she considered her death on the trip more seriously. Mia was not scared of death, not after it had come for her husband and her mother, but of course she worried about the dudes.

That was one of the biggest differences between her and the other moms, who were running around like maniacs spritzing boo-boos with sanitizer and strapping knees into pads for a skate around the block. Widows knew better. Add a dead mother to the mix and forget it.

Logistically, the dudes would be fine if Mia died—she had a will and a financial advisor thanks to her husband. He had insisted on having a will made before their younger dude was born, and stupid Mia had laughed it off, because why a will? They didn't have any money to begin with, but they were going to pay some attorney to print out a document? In the end, it was just easier to concede and so she had, and then she had never needed a piece of paper more in her life.

So if she died, which she really hoped she didn't, the boys would be okay. It was them under Ira's care that worried her. The night before he had called her elder a crybaby.

"You cannot say that to him!" she had whisper-yelled at Ira in the laundry room as he rolled his eyes.

But Mia knew that she had to let go, for her own good and the dudes' good, and so she had, with a little help from modern pharmaceutical science, and then she had slept so hard on the plane that the seat's insignia was now imprinted on her cheek.

"This way to baggage claim," Mia muttered, and followed the sign. There were two things that Mia did much more of now that she was a widow: she talked to herself, and she farted. Both incessantly.

She held her shoulders back as she crop-dusted her way up the escalator and toward her carousel. She hated that she'd had to check a bag, but if she didn't tend to her hair like a topiary in a royal garden, it looked like a neglected houseplant. When her husband had died, Mia's curls had died too.

Two hands cupped Mia's bottom from behind, and she jumped.

"George!" she yelled. The first thing she noticed was that her friend's hair did not look like a houseplant at all; it looked like it had been highlighted by Leonardo da Vinci, and probably had been. His great-nephew or something.

"Hi! Oh my God, what are you wearing? Is that a pleated jean?" George wrinkled her tiny nose in disgust.

"It's an ironic pleat."

"Really, Mia, I don't understand why you dress yourself like a librarian midwife in Maine," said George as the bags made their way out of the tunnel and dropped defeatedly onto the belt.

"That's a very specific insult," said Mia.

"Yeah, well, this whole style." George gestured toward Mia with her palm. "I know it's a thing. But why?"

George was never not bound by her clothes. Even her pajamas were tight.

"You look incredible. What did you have done?" Mia asked George, scrutinizing her glowing face.

"Oh, Todd did my eyelids. I could barely open them," she explained.

"I'm sure you could open your eyes, George," said Mia.

"Barely, I'm telling you. Maybe Todd can give you a tweak or two while you're here," George suggested. "On the house, of course."

"There's my bag," said Mia abruptly, pointing to the navy suitcase she had bought herself especially for her trip.

It sounded silly she knew, but it turned out that she couldn't bear to use her old suitcase anymore. It was part of a pair she'd shared with her husband. Traveling with her husband was the most confident Mia had ever felt. Never had she felt more desired, more his wife, more optimistic, than when they set off on an adventure together. It was the two of them versus the world. She couldn't use one without the other, and so she had given away both.

"You okay?" asked George. "I know that face."

"No," whispered Mia. "I wish everything was different."

"I know," said George. She took Mia's bag in one hand and Mia's hand in the other. "Me too."

"Your car smells like money," Mia told George.

"What does money smell like?"

"Like the ocean with a dash of the presidential rose garden and a sprinkle of muffled resentment," said Mia.

"Ever the writer," said George.

Mia settled back against the brown leather of her seat. She was here. She had made it.

"This car is only for me. I shuttle the kids around in a garbage-strewn behemoth," George explained as they merged onto the highway.

"What are they up to lately?" Chloe was eleven and Max was four. Her *happy surprise,* as George called him, which was all well and good until Max could read. *Happy surprise* was his hashtag.

"Well, Max does Mandarin, basketball, and gymnastics, and Chloe has soccer, Italian, and cooking."

"Are you kidding me?" asked Mia.

"What?"

"Are you ever not in your car?"

"See? That's why I have two. One for business and one for pleasure."

"I do that too, but with notebooks," said Mia.

"I don't mind it, really," said George. "What else am I doing?"

"Does Todd ever help out?"

"He's working."

"Weekends too?"

"Sometimes," answered George.

"And it doesn't bother you?"

"Not really," said George.

Mia considered her own childhood as she gazed out the window at California. Her dad had been a teacher, and so he had been in charge of Mia's swim meets and soccer games. He had had the time. Her mom hadn't, not really.

"I can either be grumpy at your game or happy with food waiting for you here," her mother had said to Mia when she was small, her seven-year-old legs sweating against her plastic shin guards. "Besides, we all know you're not Pelé, right?"

George's car was winding up a mountain; the skinny road on which they drove was hedged by purple, yellow, and red flowers spilling out of a sea of green like confetti. Mia opened her window. Marin County smelled like money too.

They pulled up the drive to George's three-story house, all sharp angles and windows and wood. Her door was the perfect pretentious shade of orange.

Jealousy bubbled up inside Mia like lava. She watched George saunter toward her orange door, her calves like tennis balls underneath her jeans. But she wasn't happy, Mia reminded herself. Or was she? She certainly looked happy.

The front door opened to reveal a young woman with a gigantic smile, her designer athleisure forming a precise perimeter around her perfect body.

"Hi, Selena!" said George. "So good to see you. Mia, meet

Selena, my domestic technician." George trotted past her and into the house.

"Hello," said Mia.

"Hello," Selena replied. Her youth radiated from her like a halo, and Mia felt immediate concern for her friend. There was no way that Todd didn't want to sleep with this domestic technician. Why would George bring someone this beautiful into her home? Keep your friends close and your enemies closer was one thing, but this was masochistic.

Mia nodded and trotted after George, worry churning in her empty stomach.

"Oh look, Selena has prepared us lunch!" George cooed.

Spread across a marble island were three different salads; broccoli mixed with cranberries and cashews; a sliced chicken breast with cabbage and peanuts; and a chickpea, cucumber, and tomato number. Tiny bowls of beets, pickles, and hummus were scattered throughout. When was the last time George had consumed an unapologetic carbohydrate? Maybe they were illegal here.

They sat and ate, so ravenous that neither of them spoke until all that was left on their blindingly white plates were a few errant pieces of chopped celery.

"How's the book doing?" asked George.

"I have no idea," said Mia. "I suppose I should check in with my agent."

It had been a month since its publication, and although Mia had questions, she also knew that no news was no news. Five books had taught her that.

"You haven't asked?"

"No, what's the point? It's not a bestseller. It's not even a medium seller at this point. I can tell by the Amazon reviews, of which there are only fourteen." *Fourteen.* Mia sighed.

"But isn't it being blogged about? Aren't those reviews you're posting on Instagram?"

"Yeah, but the bloggers get a free copy of the book in exchange for their posts, so it's not like I'm making any money."

"Fake it to make it," said George knowingly. "You don't post enough. Why am I not seeing you doing a giveaway? What about a partnership with a coffee brand?"

"A partnership with a coffee brand?" Mia asked. "What does that even mean?"

"Books and coffee," said George. "Coffee and parenthood. Coffee and single parenthood, no less. I mean, I assume you have to drink a gallon a day, right? Might as well get it for free."

"Too much coffee gives me diarrhea," said Mia.

"Oh. Then what about wine? Every mom loves a bottle of wine."

George posted a lot of videos of herself pouring wine into unlikely vessels: her cereal bowl for example.

"No," said Mia. "You have to be sober to read."

"Do you?" asked George as Selena cleared their plates. Her tank top shifted as she worked, revealing a stomach as tight as a drum.

"When did Selena start working for you?" she asked George.

"Six months ago. She's an au pair from Venezuela; the best decision I've ever made. She lives in the basement, which sounds bad but isn't. We renovated it last year, it's like the Ritz down there. And the kids love her. Well, Max does. Chloe doesn't like anyone." George laughed nervously. "Teenagers," she explained.

"It starts at eleven now?" asked Mia.

"It started at seven with Chloe. Todd says it's my fault."

"Well that's not nice," said Mia.

"No, it's not, but it's probably true." George sighed.

"Speaking of Todd, you're not worried about Selena? She's gorgeous."

"Oh God no," said George. "Todd is impotent."

"What?" Mia gasped. "Since when? Can't he do something about that? He's a doctor, for God's sake."

"He says he's not worried about it." George shrugged.

"Aren't you worried about it?"

"Not really," said George. "I have a vibrator. I'm fine. Several, actually."

"But what about intimacy?" asked Mia. "It's so important. I mean, why else be married?"

"This!" George extended both arms.

The George she had known had sex in the backs of cabs. She'd done anal at fourteen. Had social media taken the place of her sex life? Of course it had.

"But you used to love sex," said Mia quietly.

"I used to love a lot of things," said George. "Mia, don't look so sad! No one's dead." George covered her mouth in her hand. "Oh God, I'm an idiot. Sorry."

"It's okay," said Mia. "But you know, he is dead. I miss our intimacy probably the most of all; I missed it while he was still alive and I was too tired to do anything but sleep. Our marriage didn't work without it."

"Who said this is working?" asked George. "Our marriage just is." George's eyes were sad, but her mouth was smiling. "It's not so unusual, you know, what's happening with me and Todd. Lots of my friends don't fuck their husbands either."

Mia sat in her discomfort for a moment, twisting her cloth napkin in her lap. She had blamed her lack of interest in sex on breastfeeding and hormones, but what if she had been falling out of love? Like this?

Goddamnit. The wondering felt like it might kill Mia sometimes. She thought of her dream, the white woman with the dreadlocks. She had smelled like sex. Sex and almonds.

"Oh Mia, don't cry," said George as she reached across the table to grab her hand. "We can't all be as happy as you guys were, you know. You guys were one in a million."

"Were we? If I had known what was going to happen, I would have had more sex with him, I would have been more spontaneous, I wouldn't have nagged him the way that I had nagged him," she told George.

"Mia! Stop talking like that, right this minute. You'll kill yourself with that nonsense, do you hear me?"

"I guess I just don't understand how you can know that life is short—because you do now, George, you've seen what happened to him—and still choose to be miserable."

"Oh God, you're not here to save me from my marriage, are you?"

"What?"

"Mia, I don't need to be saved, honey. Please believe me. My marriage is not my whole life. I have the kids—well, Max—and more money than I know what to do with. I have tennis."

"Tennis?"

"Oh yeah, it's a godsend. Do you play?"

"When would I play tennis?"

"Oh for God's sake, I'll pay for a sitter, Mia. At a certain point your lack of a life outside the dudes is your fault too, you know?"

Mia dropped her napkin in her lap. She couldn't argue with George because it was true.

"Let's change the subject, shall we? How's ol' Ira doing with the dudes?" George asked as Mia stood up to clear her plate. "No, no! Sit your ass down, that's what Selena is for."

"She cooks and cleans?"

"And does the laundry," added George. "Oh, and the grocery shopping."

Mia sighed. What did George do all day, exactly?

"I'm scared to check in with Ira. I'm worried he's going to make me come home."

"No," said George. "Ira is the man. Do you remember that time he visited us in New York and dragged you to Saks to claim a gift certificate he had saved from 1978?"

"No one loves a deal more."

"Except you," said George.

It hadn't always been that way. Once when she was in college and made her own money folding sweaters at the Gap in between classes, Mia had paid retail in an ill-fated attempt to rail against her parents' frugality. Then she had run out of money. Some things you had to learn yourself.

"How does it feel to be so rich, by the way?" Mia asked George.

The last time Mia had visited George, four years prior, she

had been living in a three-bedroom apartment in San Francisco while Todd finished medical school, which was rich to be sure, but Selena and the three cars and the museum George now called a home was a different kind of rich altogether. Mia would never be this kind of rich. She was okay with that, but she was fascinated nevertheless.

"It feels pretty good," George admitted. "But wherever you go, there you are, right?"

"Right," said Mia.

"Want a tour of the house? You haven't seen this one yet, right?"

George stood up, and Mia understood that the conversation was over. She followed her, the fog-wrapped sun dappling the immaculate floor at her feet as rogue dust motes danced between its beams.

"I'm jealous," said Mia, sinking onto a white couch.

"Don't be," said George. "My husband is a eunuch, and Chloe wishes I was dead. There's nothing to be jealous about here, trust me."

George paused, then said, "I don't know what to do with her."

"Who?" asked Mia.

"Chloe."

"Therapy?"

"For two years now."

"What does Todd say?"

"He thinks I'm overreacting. Girls will be girls, he says, which has merit until your daughter wields her cutlery like a weapon."

"I'm so sorry, George," said Mia. "I hated my parents too, but not until high school." She thought of her mother and all the horrible things she had said to her. They had forgiven each other, but not without effort and not until much later.

"I never hated mine, is the thing," said George. "Probably because they let me do whatever I wanted. Oh, you look so pretty in this light, let me get a picture."

"Oh God, you're shooting me head-on?" asked Mia. "Give me an angle, please."

"No, no, we can't do that. Then it will look like you're trying too hard. It has to be head-on or underneath."

"Underneath! You're a monster," said Mia, laughing.

"Listen, I don't make the rules," said George, snapping away. "And no filter."

"How terrifying. You can't post that."

"I can and I will," said George. "Someone has to do your publicity. And you look beautiful, so shut it. See?"

Mia cringed as she beheld herself on George's screen. She looked old, but she also looked like she didn't care that she was old.

"Why do you do all this stuff?" she asked George.

"What stuff?"

"The posting?"

"I dunno. It's fun? It validates my existence?"

"Are you okay, though? I know when I'm posting a lot, I'm in the weeds."

"Of course I'm not okay. Is anyone okay? And what's the problem with posting? I'm not hurting anybody, am I?"

George was technically right. The happy photos of her doting husband who never touched her, her soccer-playing daughter with an orange slice in her mouth instead of a butter knife in her hand—they didn't hurt anyone. But they didn't help anyone either.

"No," said Mia.

"They're just pictures," said George with a catch in her voice. "Don't judge me."

"I'm not."

"You are."

"I'm not! I'm just worried about you."

"Stop worrying." She glared at Mia.

"So where is the fam?" asked Mia, accepting George's terms. Did that make her a bad friend or a good friend? she wondered. With a twenty-one-year-old friendship, it was hard to know.

"Chloe is horseback riding, and Max is at Mandarin," answered George. "It's the language of the future, you know. He's out back in the guesthouse with his tutor, Jian. That's where you'll be staying, by the way. If it's okay with you, that is."

Mia stood up and walked over to the ten-foot windows overlooking the saltwater pool. On the back of the property stood another home.

"Hell yeah, it's okay with me."

"I made us appointments for massages at two," said George.

"I feel like I'm in a dream," said Mia.

"Good," said George.

MIA PULLED A cigarette from her pack. She had been a smoker almost all her life, which was disgusting and shameful and stupid, but she had stopped when she was pregnant with her first child. Then after he was born and very casually at first, her husband would bum a cigarette from a twenty-something on the rare occasions that they were out actually socializing in public instead of watching their son sleep on the baby monitor: *Is he facedown? I can't tell! Should I go in? No, you go in! Fine, I'll go in!* and so forth.

The difference between Mia and her husband, however—one of them, at least—was that she was an addict and he was not. He could smoke a cigarette on a Saturday night and not think about it again, but Mia would have a cigarette on a Saturday night and find herself at a bodega at seven A.M. the next morning, asking for a lighter too.

She had became a secret smoker, smoking when her kids napped sometimes, but always followed by a shower. Her husband had had the nose of a bloodhound. He had known, or hadn't he? Mia wasn't sure, but that had been the thrill all along, she guessed. Something just for her, never mind that it was killing her. A full-time mother was never allowed to be alone unless she was spewing noxious fumes of smoke from her nostrils, and so she had done what she had to do. At least that was what Mia had told herself once upon a time, when she had a husband. Now she smoked all the time, hiding unsuccessfully behind a scraggly fir tree in the backyard to keep it from the dudes, but really who the fuck cared. Her husband had been the guy who washed every vegetable, who never microwaved plastic, who always got the side salad, who only smoked one cigarette a year, and still death had come for him.

She'd been able to hide it from the dudes for a bit, disguising her habit with a trash compulsion.

"I'm taking out the recycling!" she would call to them as they sat transfixed by the tablets she had bought them, because who needed to pay a babysitter when YouTube existed?

"I'm taking out the glass bottles!"

"I'm taking out the compost!"

They didn't compost.

Her elder had caught on, sobbing hysterically in the backyard as Mia promised that she would quit but knowing that she wouldn't. She didn't think she wanted to die, but yet there she was killing herself. The truth was that she thought she might get a pass in terms of cancer since the universe had already screwed her over so royally, but even as she thought it, she knew that the universe did not specialize in fair. She had to stop. She would. She just had to do it already, she always finished what she started, that was the Mia Macher way.

"When I get home, I'll quit," she announced. There, she had said it.

She stubbed her cigarette out now in George's perfectly manicured lawn and flushed it down the extraordinarily clean commode. It was a very real fear of Mia's that she would set something on fire, and so she disposed of her cigarette butt immediately in the first body of water she saw, which was always a bathroom, since Mia never, ever smoked in public. Then everyone would know how disgusting she was, and she couldn't have that.

Mia spritzed a cloud of perfume from a white porcelain bottle, swished a generous mouthful of Scope, and slathered her hands with a coconut-and-lemon-scented lotion perched over the sink.

The dudes, she thought. Her father. She should call.

Her elder picked up the phone.

"Mom!" he said, and smiled his father's smile.

Next Mia saw the wood floor of her house and then the couch and then, finally, her younger son's face.

"Mom!" he echoed, and smiled her smile. "Where are you?" he demanded.

"I'm in California," she answered. "At George's house."

"Who is George?" he asked, his cherubic face scrunched up quizzically.

"George! The one who bought you McDonald's," she explained for the fifty-eighth time.

"Ohhhhhhhh," he replied, nodding in recognition.

The screen whizzed past the built-in bookcases flanking the French doors that overlooked a mud pit masquerading as a backyard, a yard with so much potential and zero interest from Mia although plenty of interest from every squirrel in the tristate area.

"Mom is with the McDonald's lady!" her younger informed her elder, handing him the phone.

"Is that her house?" he asked, craning his neck as though the phone's frame was just a suggestion.

"It's her guesthouse," she informed him.

"Whoa, she's rich."

"Yeah, she is. Look, there are two showerheads," she continued, extending her arm into the very generous stall.

"Are those golden?" asked her younger.

"Yep," said Mia. She flopped down on the king-size bed and sunk into its comforter.

"How are you guys doing?" she asked them. Both of their faces were crowded into the screen.

"Good," they answered in unison.

"Mom, can Grandpa and me get tattoos?" asked her elder.

"What? And it's 'Grandpa and I,' not 'Grandpa and me.' You wouldn't say, 'Can me get a tattoo,' would you? And no, you cannot get tattoos. Where is Grandpa, by the way?"

"He's in the bathroom!" squealed her younger, and the phone once again roller coastered through her living room.

"No! No! I don't want to see him in the bathroom!" Mia screamed. "Please!"

In front of the wonky door that never truly closed, the phone stopped and Ira shuffled out. It was always a shock for Mia to realize that her father was old, but of course he was. She was old.

"Hello, Mia," he yelled, holding the phone three inches from his face.

"Dad, I'm right here, you don't have to yell."

"Oh, sorry," he said.

"How's it going? Are they being jerky?" asked Mia.

"No, we're having a ball. Right, guys?"

Silence.

"Forget about them. They're fine."

"Tonight is movie night!" yelled her younger from the background.

"How are you, Dad? Are you okay?" asked Mia.

"Sure, why not. They keep me on my toes."

Her elder grabbed the phone.

"Grandpa made us go on a forty-five-minute walk today!" he complained. "I was so hungry."

"I like to take my time," said Ira. "I'm seventy-three, I can do what I want."

"He made us do trivia!" the younger screamed in protest.

"Oh, Dad, you didn't," said Mia.

"Your sons are good boys, but they're lazy," Ira told her plainly.

All of Mia's childhood, whenever they found themselves waiting in the car for her mother, her father would pepper her with trivia questions and pop-up spelling bees. On one unfortunate occasion he had asked her what the capital of Russia was, to which she had replied, "Little Rock." It had become a running joke.

"Sure, she can write a book, but does she know what the capital of Russia is?" Ira would say to whoever was listening.

"It's good for them," he told her now.

"Just go easy on them."

"You're too easy on them, if you ask me," Ira said. "But you're the boss."

"Dad, their father died. Give them a break."

"Careful now, that's a dangerous way to raise your kids. The world isn't going to care that their dad died, Mia."

"That's exactly why I'm caring now."

Mia sighed. It was a delicate balance between heartbreak on their behalf and raising entitled pricks—she knew that. But she was trying.

"Have they eaten any vegetables?" Mia asked her father.

"Check."

"Are they pooping?"

"And how."

"Washing their hands?"

"Of course."

"Thank you. Really, Dad. Thank you. It's so nice to be away."

"You're welcome. How's George?"

"Loaded. Lost. She doesn't even like her husband, much less love him. What's the point?"

"Every couple goes through that," said Ira. "I didn't like your mother all of the time."

"No, but you loved her." Mia paused. "Right?"

"Of course. But she was a piece of work. You know that. Judy is . . . easier."

"What a compliment," said Mia.

"You know what? It is at our age."

Mia lay back on the bed and stared at the ceiling fan over her head. Her mother would have eaten Judy for lunch.

"I really needed this trip," she told her dad. "Thank you."

"Stop thanking me already," said Ira. In the background she heard the dudes revving up and knew that they would soon be wrestling through the living room and up the stairs, from bed to bed and down again, screaming, "STOP!" over and over again until Ira's ears bled.

"You are coming back?" Ira asked. "Right?"

CHAPTER 8

MIA OPENED HER EYES TO DARKNESS. SHE hadn't set her phone alarm, but her body was a creature of habit and so at two A.M. Californian Utopian Time, there she was, rolled into a thousand-thread-count sheet burrito and wide awake.

When she woke up like this under normal circumstances, she would write, or at the very least sit down at her desk and pour a gallon of coffee down her throat before the dudes woke up and jolted her back to them.

She had this same window of freedom at the end of the day too, of course, after she had sent the dudes to bed under penalty of death, but by that point her brain was nothing but bubbling slime. All Mia could manage to do was fold laundry in front of bankrupt former gold diggers masquerading as entrepreneurs on the television while drinking more wine than she needed. Drinking never felt as good after the first glass. There was no point, and yet Mia found herself refilling once, sometimes two times, and for what? If her husband was still alive, there was no way she would be drinking like this, but maybe that was the point.

Today, Mia could write, she supposed, but the idea for her next novel didn't have legs yet—well, it didn't have a contract yet, to be honest, and so the impetus was minimal at best. But she had to get that contract; she had to keep writing, because writing was the love of her life. It always had been.

No matter what phase Mia was going through—funny girl, anorexic girl, stoner girl, single twenty-something in Brooklyn girl, married woman girl, mother—it was her only constant. Her writing kept her sane.

And to think that she had somehow managed to get paid for it! To write books that were bound and published! That people read her work and felt less alone. It was a miracle.

Mia had always known she would be a writer, which seemed like a big deal to most people but was really so simple. Mia's soul sang when she wrote, and through the rest of the process too—even when it seemed impossible, especially when it seemed impossible. Through all the edits and edits and edits and even through the swirling black hole of doubt that always lurked nearby, threatening to pull her in at any moment, she loved it.

The impossibility of turning her idea into four hundred pages was possible. And if that was possible, then anything was possible. Writing was Mia's superpower.

What if, Mia wondered now, wrapped in George's cold, buttery sheets, everyone left the womb with their superpower spelled out for them? On a sheet of parchment rolled into their tiny fist?

Her husband:

You will die when you are forty-four. You will be young and beautiful and full of life and vitality and it will make sense to no one. *Your superpower is your heart; it is as infinite as the ocean. Follow it.*

Their elder:

Your father will die when you are five. You will keep him alive in both mind and heart because he will pass these parts of himself on to you. Your superpower is your emotional fluency. Use it for good.

Their younger:

Your father will die two days after you turn two. Your mom will cry all the time, but know that she is breaking herself down in order to put herself back together. Your superpower is your focus. Pick your path with care.

The room turned apricot with promise as Mia's eyes leaked down her face. Even when she was happy, she was sad, and that was just how widowhood was going to be. Mia's acceptance of this felt like a medal she had earned from battle.

#FunWidow indeed.

Was it all planned from the beginning? Was that what God did? How could God have done that to her husband, then? There was so much that he hadn't gotten to see, so much he had yet to learn. It had never been *why her?* for Mia, but it would always be *why him?*

That next morning, after his brain had flooded with blood, after Mia had sat with him all night and watched that blood drain into a bag next to his bed, she had come home from the hospital to have breakfast with the dudes. She had splashed water on her gray face, behind the closed door of the bathroom. The feeling of being alive when he wasn't crushed her, and she had leaned heavily against the sink. The lights had flickered. She'd looked up, her eyes so dry they felt like wool—and then they had flickered again.

"I love you," she had heard her husband say. "I'm sorry."

"It's not your fault," Mia had whispered. "Don't be sorry."

Mia had been raised to equate God with the soul. She knew no other way to explain miracles. But there was just no way to make sense of his death.

What Mia wouldn't give to not be thinking about the existential infrastructure at two o'clock in the morning. What she wouldn't give to think that what had happened to her husband was the kind of thing that happened to other people and not to him. To her. To them. She pulled herself tighter into the cocoon of George's bedding and waited for sleep.

"OH, HI," MIA mumbled, her mouth filled with bagel and lox.

She was sitting at the marble island of George's kitchen. The house had been empty as far as Mia had been able to tell when she had first padded in on bare feet in a black sweatshirt that read "NO" across its front.

Now Todd stood before her, zipped into a red fleece, a lone squash-shaped island of hair on his otherwise balding head. He looked pleased with himself in the way that wealthy men did, no doubt free balling in his designer shorts, because who needed underwear when someone else did the laundry?

"Hey, Mia, glad you got to sleep in," said Todd. "It's nice out there, right?" Gray stubble rimmed his jaw.

She shouldn't be so hard on him. He wasn't her husband, for God's sake.

Mind your business, her mother would have told her.

"It's beautiful out there," she answered. "Just to have all that space to myself! Oy."

She peered at Todd as he hovered over the breakfast platter, folding pink ribbons of lox into his mouth one by one.

Mia sometimes daydreamed about having her entire face ripped off so she could grow a new one. The sunspots, the wrinkles, the circles, her eyelids like Silly Putty, the beginnings of her fated turkey neck—it shocked her in the mirror most mornings. But to erase all of it felt disrespectful. She was a forty-three-year-old widow. She was what that looked like. She had survived. To erase the evidence would have been missing the point entirely.

Still, she was acutely aware of her low-hanging nipples in her thin sweatshirt. She put down her coffee mug so that she could fold her arms over her chest. Todd must look at her the way an auto mechanic looked at an old car, she thought. But then she realized that Todd wasn't looking at her at all. He was scrolling through his phone. She uncrossed her arms.

When George had asked Mia to be a bridesmaid, she had almost said no on principle—she had always thought that George could do better than Todd—but had ended up marching down the aisle in an ill-fitting shantung two-piece abomination with the rest of them.

That was thanks to her mother, who had said, *Oh for God's sake, you're going to make this woman's wedding about you, Mia? Get over yourself,* when Mia had called her to complain. Mia missed her mother's voice most of all.

"You dating yet?" Todd asked Mia now, bringing her out from

offstage. That was what it felt like when she was in her head with her memories, watching them unfurl from the wings.

"No," she answered from behind a monogrammed napkin.

"Dad!" yelled a girl's voice, and Mia shivered. That word.

It seemed to be a law of nature that little girls born to beautiful mothers looked like their fathers. Chloe was Todd in miniature: solid in stature, slightly bowlegged, chinless. Her eyebrows appeared translucent on her face. The only nod to George spilled out of an elastic on top of Chloe's head in white-blonde waves down her back.

"Hi, Chloe," said Mia. "Holy cow, I can't believe how much you've grown! You're a young woman."

"Hi," she said, her bored eyes reading Mia's chest. "And I'm not a woman."

"You're not?"

"I'm a they."

"Oh," said Mia. "Sorry. You're a young they."

Mia was not fluent in modern gender language. She had heard rumors about he/she/they, but reading about it made her head hurt. *Pick a lane*, her father's voice told her.

This was her initial response too, until she thought about who had made the lanes in the first place. Old white men on a mountain in the desert? And who knew whom the dudes were going to be once they understood their options? She would roll with it. Other people's pronouns weren't about her.

"Dad, I'm hungry," Chloe told Todd.

"Oh," he answered. "Where's Selena?"

"It's Sunday," said Chloe.

"Oh. Well, make yourself a bowl of cereal or something. You can do that, can't you?"

"Chloe!" a raspy boy voice yelled as it boomed and thudded down the stairs and into the kitchen.

"Hi, Max," said Mia, feeling the sharp pang in her uterus of missing her dudes. Was there anything cuter than a shirtless boy just out of bed?

"Hi?" he answered. "Who are you?"

"I'm Mia, your mom's friend. I haven't seen you since you were a baby." Max looked like his mama, with blonde curls tickling his golden cheeks, the bone structure of a Grecian god, and a five-pack of stomach muscles. Poor Chloe.

"Could I walk?" he asked.

"What do you mean?" asked Mia.

"When you saw me and I was a baby?"

"No, I don't think so. I'm pretty sure you just sat."

"Could I talk?"

"No, except maybe words like 'gaggagoogoobutt.'" Max's brown eyes lit up like slot machines as he considered Mia's newfound potential. "Where's your mom?" she asked Chloe.

"Playing tennis with the girls," Chloe recited. They clutched their rib cage dramatically. "I'm starving!"

Todd plucked another ribbon of lox from the platter and folded it into his mouth.

"Ew, Dad, gross," said Chloe.

"Well, can I make you guys bagels?" Mia asked. It was abundantly clear that Todd wasn't going to be getting involved in feeding his children, which did not surprise Mia as much as it repulsed her.

She proceeded to toast and not toast; schmear and scoop; place and pour until Chloe and Max were happily chewing, feet swinging on Lucite barstools. Todd had taken up residence on the couch, his bare feet propped on a pillow like bunny ears.

"Hi!" yelled George finally as the front door clicked closed. "I'm back!" She surfed into the kitchen on a wave of sunscreen and orange blossom.

"Mia!"

Underneath her visor, Mia could see that George wasn't wearing any makeup. She looked younger and older at the same time.

"Is that a tennis skirt?"

"Indeed it is. I'm mostly in it for the fashion."

"What else is new?" mumbled Todd.

"I see you've reconnected with Todd," George said, and fluttered around her children like a butterfly, hugging and cleaning errant crumbs with her wings.

"Mom!" said Chloe. "That's my face!"

"Yes, so tennis," George continued. "I started playing a year or so ago, I think? The girls and I took lessons together and then we joined a league. It's good exercise. I'm not great, but I'm not bad either."

"She got a trophy!" Max proudly volunteered.

"Get out, you have trophies?" asked Mia.

"Oh yeah, it's super cute, every spring we have a banquet, everybody gets dressed up and hammered. It's fun."

"Wow, this is a whole thing," said Mia.

Who were these girls George played with? she wondered. She had never heard about them before. She wondered if they were all married like George was and figured they probably were. Mom widows didn't have time for tennis.

"Good for you," she told George sincerely. "You look great."

"Thanks." George looked at her, really looked at her, and Mia sensed a sadness in her, a sadness that even her sculpted and pore-less face couldn't hide. What did it feel like to be George? Mia wondered.

"What are we doing today?" Max asked her as he licked the cream cheese off his bagel, smearing it on the tip of his nose and chin in the process.

"We're not doing anything," George told him. "Mia and I are going to head down to the beach and walk around, get a light lunch before her event tonight. Oysters and champagne, anyone?" she offered, plucking a blueberry from Max's plate.

"Just one glass," said Mia.

"Oh, come on," said George.

"I have to be almost sober for my reading. Two is too many but one is my requirement," Mia explained.

"Okay, you're going to shower, right?" George picked a sesame bagel off the tray and began to claw out its contents with her fingers, their coral tips coated in crumbs. "And for God's sake, put on a bra."

"Could this place be more spectacular? Is it real? Are we dead?" asked Mia, her toes buried in the damp sand.

Stinson Beach backed right up into the mountains, the water lapping at the wild grass of their base. Mia had never seen any-thing like it, having grown up on the East Coast, where moun-tains and beaches were separate entities entirely.

"It's pretty amazing, right?" asked George. They were the only ones there, for miles and sandy miles.

"So how are you feeling about tonight?" asked George. She had a blue-and-white gingham scarf tied over her blonde hair, the glossy ends of which danced around her shoulders in the wind.

"I'm okay. Nothing in my life looks anything like I thought it would look like, but I'm okay."

"You mean because you're a widow?"

"Yeah. Like, I have two kids. By myself. My husband fucking died." Mia sighed and shook her head. "I'm just trying to figure out who I'm going to be now, you know? Is this the new version of me, and if not, what the fuck is next?"

"Just like Felicity," said George.

Felicity was a show they had watched together religiously as roommates, sitting in a fog of bong smoke on their inherited couch, a batch of just-made, still slightly raw chocolate chip cookies still warm on the coffee table.

"Yeah, but instead of choosing between Ben and Noel, I'm choosing between . . . what am I choosing between?"

"You're choosing between the past and the future. It's like, you can either consider your marriage the best thing that ever happened to you, or you can manifest the fact that the best is yet to come," said George.

"Oh God, not this manifest bullshit."

"You don't buy it?"

"It's not that I don't buy it, I just hate the commercialization of it. It's like, no, you don't just *build it and it will come.* My credit card bill is proof of that. Keep your mouth shut and just do the work."

"You're very passionate about this," said George.

"Yeah, well, it's such commercialized bullshit."

"True," said George. "But manifesting isn't hurting anybody, so why not?"

"I guess?" said Mia, thinking. "But actually, no. It is hurting people. All of the people who don't make good on their dream? What do they have to say about manifesting?" Cold water tickled Mia's toes, and she jumped slightly. "Why, what are you manifesting?"

"Oh man," said George with a heavy sigh. "I don't know. I feel so stuck."

"How?" asked Mia, excited about the fact that George was finally letting her in. Something the dudes' therapist had told her once was to let them come to her with their feelings instead of imposing her own. It was good advice.

"I know you think I'm pathetic," she told Mia.

"I absolutely do not! What are you talking about?"

"I can see it on your face. You have very judgy eyes."

"Judgy eyes!" Mia's mother had had the same eyes. "I'm sorry, I was born with them. But I've never, ever thought of you as pathetic, George. That's you putting your shit on me. What is that called again?"

"Transference," answered George. "Okay, so what do you think of me as, then?"

Mia thought. In her mind, she saw George at twenty-three,

standing up in their kitchen and eating peanut noodles from a white paper container. She saw her on the 6 train, holding the door back to let Mia on. She saw George holding her father's hand on Fourteenth Street, walking into the sunset toward a fancy dinner to which Mia had been invited. She saw her crying over an unwanted pregnancy, rolled into her toile comforter, facing the window of her bedroom wall, a window that looked right into the kitchen of a Chinese restaurant.

"I think of you as complicated," said Mia. "That's why I love you so much."

"Is that a nicer word for crazy?"

"No, not at all. It means that you're so much more than who you appear to be. On the surface you're like this girl next door if you live in a rich neighborhood, but you're also so much more than that. You're funny and smart. You're generous and kind. I mean, honestly, George, is this the life you want? Your husband is impotent and doesn't know how to make bagels for your kids."

"Oh no, don't start," said George.

"It's a bagel, George. Literally you just spread something on it with a knife and slap it together."

George walked quietly beside her, watching her feet move through the wet sand.

"Do you love him?"

"No."

"Then why do you stay?"

"I don't like being alone," George told her.

"But you are alone," said Mia. "Do you even see Todd? The way you tell it, you and the kids have totally separate lives."

"We do," said George.

"So why stay? You have the choice to leave. Life is so fucking short, George. You don't have to be unhappy."

"Because maybe it's not him that makes me unhappy? What if I get out and then I'm still miserable? And broke to boot?"

"I'm not broke, and that's a goddamn miracle," Mia told her. "You would have to get a job, though."

"Gross," said George. "I'm kidding. Sort of. But what about the kids? I couldn't do that to them."

"Do what?" asked Mia.

"Divorce their dad."

Mia felt her face go hot. She hated it when parents blamed their kids for their own complacency.

"That's bullshit, George, and you know it."

"It's actually not. What kind of message is it to send that when the going gets tough, you bail?"

"What kind of message is it to send that you accept less than you're worth?" Mia shot back.

"I don't want to be a single parent. It looks horrible!" yelled George. She stopped walking and put her hands on her white denim hips.

"It is horrible," agreed Mia. "It's like running a fucking marathon every single day. But I'm proud of myself. And the dudes can sense that."

"You think Chloe would be nicer to me if I left their father?"

"Maybe? I always wished my parents would get a divorce."

"You did?"

Mia's parents had argued throughout her childhood. But when

she had left for college, something had shifted in her absence. They had learned to love each other again. But eighteen years of pain hardly seemed worth it.

"I didn't mean that your life looks horrible, Mia. Just hard. It looks hard."

"If horrible to you is knowing how to do absolutely everything, then yes, it's horrible."

"Yuck," said George.

"It's a choice to not see it that way," said Mia. "Some days are easier than others. But it feels good to be this capable, I gotta tell you, George. Like, I'm not worried. About anything. I know I can do anything."

"I always thought you could do anything," said George. "Even before all of this."

"Well, I couldn't. And if I can become a person who can handle anything, then you certainly can, George. I'm not special.

"I swear I'm not judging you, George," said Mia. "I just want the best for you. Truly."

"I get what you're saying. I know that our marriage is not a marriage at all. But the rest of my life is fine. Better than fine. I have the best clothes, the best surgery, the best kids—well, Max is the best, Chloe has always been a pain in the ass." She sighed. "It's not so bad, Mia."

Mia couldn't bear to hear her friend be so trapped by her wealth. She couldn't relate.

"I manifested my marriage," Mia told her.

"I know you did," George said, and took Mia's hand.

Mia had always known that her husband was the one. She

couldn't explain it, but she had known it from the first moment she had seen his face. She knew he was someone who had meant something to her at some point and would mean something to her again—she knew it in her heart in a way she had never known anything. Well, almost anything. Mia Macher was going to be an author—she had always known that too.

"Remember when you met him?" asked George. "You had just gotten your first book deal."

"That's right. And then there he was."

"There he was," echoed George. She bent down to pull a gray freckled shell from the sand. "Wow, look at this. It's perfect. Maybe I'll have it strung."

"You would never have that strung," said Mia. "You aren't a shell-stringing kind of person."

"You're right." She tossed it into the froth nipping at their toes and looked at her watch, which peeked out from an artful stack of gold bangles.

"We should turn around. I'm getting hungry," she said.

Mia followed George back the way they had come, through the sand as the sun broke through the mass of gray clouds overhead. George was broken in a way that Mia couldn't fix. The kind of fixing that had to come from within.

George stopped walking suddenly and turned to Mia.

"He's not impotent, by the way. It's just what I tell people."

"What? Why would you lie to me about that?"

"I'm embarrassed. We just don't want to have sex with each other, but we're perfectly capable of having actual sex. And I've seen him look at Selena."

"George!" said Mia. "Why would you bring her into your home, then?"

"I don't know? To test him?"

"God." Mia shook her head and sighed. "And what if he fails the test?"

"Then I have to get out," answered George. "Then I have no choice."

"But why put yourself in that position?"

"Because then I would get the kids. And the money. It's the perfect crime."

"Wouldn't you get the kids anyway?" asked Mia.

"Todd comes from a long line of lawyers. He'd get the kids and the house and the other house—"

"There's another house?"

"In Park City, yes."

"Utah? What the hell are you doing with a house in Utah?"

"Todd has to be on call during Sundance," George explained.

"What?"

"Oh yeah, these celebrities could deflate at any moment."

"Jesus," said Mia. She took George's hand. "Why did you lie to me about Todd's impotency? I'm your best friend. I've waxed your vagina, for God's sake."

George smiled. "Sometimes you get so used to the lie that the truth doesn't even occur to you anymore," she told Mia.

"I know."

Mia told herself lies all the time just to get through the day: that she was the nanny waiting for the dudes' real parents to come home and relieve her; that she didn't have anything useful to say so why bother saying or writing it at all; that she was overweight. The lies were survival tactics meant to keep her from trying harder, because if she tried any harder she would fall over and die.

Mia tugged George toward the water's edge with her, letting it splash the cuffs of their jeans before it pulled away, leaving a faint rim of foam in its wake.

"Don't you miss sex?" she asked George. "I do."

"You can have sex any time you want, Mia. You don't have to miss it, you know."

"I know. But I don't want to have it with anyone but him." A pelican plunged its pouch into the waves and then emerged, victorious.

"Anyway, my vagina is like a black hole now anyway," offered Mia. "The dudes ruined me on their way out."

"Well, Todd can fix that."

"Gross," said Mia.

"Think about it." Mia rolled her eyes. "I'm serious!"

They were off the beach now and almost to the parking lot.

"Hey, do you remember our shithole apartment?" George asked.

"Animal Kingdom," said Mia.

There had been roaches in the cabinets, rats in the walls, and pigeons in the shower. Mia's appreciation for her dwellings thereafter, for her slow but steady climb upward, had roots.

"I still can't believe you lived there with me. You're rich. You belonged on the Upper East Side."

"My father was making a point. He didn't want me in New York, so he didn't pay for anything. Until I came home."

"I know, but that was mean," said Mia.

"Was it? I learned a lot. Like that rats can gnaw off their own legs, for example."

"Those useless glue traps. I got stuck in one every other day," said Mia. "Remember our jobs? Oh God, our bosses."

George had spent most of her days buying cocaine and scheduling blowouts for her twenty-eight-year-old boss. Mia had worked in advertising doing pretty much the same thing, but for a middle-aged man.

"God, I got so fat in that apartment," said Mia.

"You did gain a lot of weight," said George. "But I wouldn't have called you fat. Matronly, maybe?"

"Fuck you."

Mia could feel the stagnant summer air, smell the rotting garbage that spilled out of every corner's receptacle that summer she had decided to start eating again, her first summer after college graduation.

She had been lost in the West Village, standing on a corner that was supposed to be Eighth Street but wasn't. Everywhere she'd looked was an impossibly thin and beautiful person: buying cigarettes at the bodega, drinking white wine with their denim-clad legs crossed, walking their French bulldogs. They were everywhere, and Mia was struck, as if by lightning, by the notion that she had better get cracking on her insides, because her outsides weren't that great. Not by New York standards, anyway. Inside, she was funny. Inside, she was vulnerable. Inside, she was a writer.

So she had gained thirty pounds in six months but hadn't written a thing. It turned out that eating, if you were Mia, took up a lot of time. Not the act of it so much as the obsessing about it. She may have "cured" herself on the outside, but the inside was still a mess.

"You couldn't pay me to go back to my twenties," she told George now.

"You did lose the weight, though. Eventually."

Mia had spent the twenty-seventh year of her life weighing in on Tuesdays at 8:35 A.M.

"Weight Watchers," she told George.

All her life she had never known how to eat. As a kid, sugar was forbidden, so of course she had sought it out. As a teenager, she had been miserable in her strong body, but not miserable enough to do anything about it. Until college. Away at college for the first time in her life, out of the grip of her parents, she had been overwhelmed by her freedom. So she had controlled the only thing she could. Food.

"Weight Watchers, Shmeight Watchers. You fixed yourself. You always do."

Mia's work ethic came from Ira. *If you're going to do it, do it right,* he had taught her. Solid advice for Mia's schoolwork; not so solid for her addictive tendencies.

"I guess," said Mia.

"You've always done hard with such grace," said George. "It's like you were born to do hard."

"Great," said Mia. What she wouldn't give to do easy for a change. Although even as she thought this, she knew it wasn't true. Easy wasn't her nature, George was right.

"I don't do hard. But you! You do hard. You specialize in hard. You always have," George continued.

"But don't you think that you signed up for hard when you de-cided to become a mother?" asked Mia.

"It's only as hard as you want it to be," said George.

"Or you can afford it to be," countered Mia.

"Same thing."

"You can do hard," Mia told George. "Remember when you moved to L.A.? You didn't know a soul."

"I lasted three and a half months living on my own in Malibu and then I met Todd. I wouldn't call that hard."

"Why are you so mean to yourself?" Mia asked her. "You're so good to your outsides—what about your insides?"

"I'm not mean, I'm just honest. I'm forty-three years old, Mia. I know who I am."

They grabbed their sandals, smacking their soles together as they approached George's car.

"I know you could do hard. I know you would surprise your-self. But you have to want it first."

"Exactly," said George, unlocking her door and climbing in.

"You make me mad," Mia admitted as they drove away.

"Why?"

"Because I don't think you're happy, and you deserve to be happy."

"Why can't I just be someone who's happy enough?" asked George.

"I guess you can be," said Mia. "I'll still love you regardless. But it makes me mad."

"Okay," said George. "Thanks for loving me anyway."

"You're welcome," said Mia.

CHAPTER 9

MIA SAT BY THE POOL. CALIFORNIA WAS TOO beautiful. She didn't have the stamina to live there. And anyway, she liked being inside. Inside her home, inside her head, inside her characters.

She called her father.

"Hello," he answered. "Why didn't you call me on the FaceThing?"

"I thought I might catch you alone."

"For what?"

"To catch up."

"Since when do you and I catch up?"

"I want to know how the dudes are doing without them listening in, okay, Dad? Jesus."

"Oh, well, you're in luck because you caught me in the john. It's the only place where they don't bother me."

"Tell me about it," said Mia.

She uncrossed and then recrossed her shins, which were turning an alarming shade of pink in the sun.

"Dad, it's crazy here—the mountains tumble right down into the water," she told him.

"Wow," he said. "Your mother and I went there once, when you were small. Do you remember?"

"Did Grandma stay with me?" she asked.

"Sure did."

"I remember."

Mia's grandmother, her mother's mother. They had watched Bette Davis movies together and eaten birthday cake for breakfast. It had been a long time since she had thought of her grandmother. So many other dead people had taken precedence.

Sorry, Grandma.

"You and Mom drove the coast, right?"

Mia remembered her parents coming home with a stuffed sea lion for her. Her disappointment. She had wanted Michael J. Fox's autograph.

"We sure did. It doesn't get more beautiful than that, let me tell you."

"How old were you?"

"A little younger than you are now," he told her. Mia thought about her parents in their forties and then thought about herself in her forties.

They had been married with a daughter. She was a widow with two sons. They had had nine-to-five jobs without email. She took her laptop wherever she went, and if she didn't answer a text, she had told George, Rachel, and Chelsea to assume that she was dead.

"Did your marriage change, Dad? After I was born?"

"Oh yeah," he said. "Your mother was so tired. She worked full time."

"I remember, Dad, I was there."

"Don't be a wiseass," he told her.

"Did you reconnect on that trip?"

Mia and her husband had never gotten to take a trip alone together after the dudes were born. Mia hadn't wanted to leave them. What a fool she had been.

"We had a nice time."

Mia wondered often what her marriage would have looked like, now that the dudes were fully functioning humans. The hardest part was trying to remember what it felt like to be part of a team. She could see it in her mind, but she couldn't feel it in her heart. It was terribly disconcerting.

"Are you really okay, Dad?" she asked, swallowing her tears. "Do you need me to come home? Because I can come home." The words spilled out of Mia before she could catch them.

"Whoa, whoa, whoa, take it easy," said Ira. "I'm fine, we're fine."

"Dad, really?"

"Mia, we're only a day and some change into this thing. Relax. Listen, the big guy is too sensitive and the little one never stops yelling, but they're good boys. You're doing a great job with them, Mia."

Mia was only proud of herself when her father was proud of her; that was the way it had always been.

"Thanks, Dad," she warbled, her voice thick.

"Hey, Dad?"

"Yeah?"

"Where did your grief go?"

"What do you mean?"

"You moved on with Judy so quickly. Where did it go?"

Had she ever asked him outright? She didn't think so.

"Mia, I'm going to tell you something." Her toilet flushed in New Jersey. "Hold on a second."

A hummingbird hovered, and Mia marveled at the way its wings worked triple time to keep it aloft.

"You people today with grief this and grief that," Ira continued. "Where I come from, you just get on with things. Because what other choice do you have? I never stopped loving your mother. I never stopped missing her. But that was it. She was gone. And it was a blessing too, Mia. She was so sick."

Her mother had been diagnosed with pancreatic cancer in June of her sixty-sixth year. By that November, she was gone.

"And she wanted me to remarry too; she told me that, Mia. She knew who I was and what I needed. She wanted me to be happy."

Mia closed her eyes. She was eight years old and walking home from school. Her mother, surprising her at the top of the hill, a swirl of shiny brown hair and white teeth and pleats. Loafers on her feet. Laughing. Her warm, dry hand.

"Maybe it's never been about Mom at all," Mia admitted now.

Mia listened to the breeze moving through the trees, the birds chirping in their branches. She closed her eyes and was thirty-six again, pulling her mother up from the hospital bed to help her to the bathroom, her once-strong legs like matchsticks, her ribs showing through her gown. Her brown eyes like open windows.

It was too sad to remember her mother poised on the precipice of her own demise. Awake. Aware. Okay with their after without her.

"Write about me," her mother had told her from her wheelchair. They were outside on the screened-in porch; the air finally cool after the eternal Georgia summer. "Since I'll be dead, you can say whatever you want."

"Mom!"

"What? I mean it. You have my permission."

Wasn't that just like a mother, to keep giving even when she was gone?

"Finally," said Ira now. "Is that an apology?"

"Maybe."

"Where are the dudes?" she asked her father, and wiped her face with the back of her hand. "It's too quiet there."

"They're on their screen things. Mia, honestly, the garbage they watch."

"I know." Mia sighed.

"So your big reading is tonight, huh? You're gonna be great. Just don't wear that horrible dress," her father advised.

Mia had worn what in retrospect was a horrible dress, but at the time was a more-than-suitable—as well as very expensive—dress to the first reading she had ever given. It was short and leopard-printed with puffy shoulders that tickled her earlobes and a bodice that had smashed her relatively ample bosom into a pancake.

"Those shoulders on it!" He made a gagging noise. "You looked like a linebacker."

"Grandpa!" her younger yelled, saving her.

"I'm coming, I'm coming!" her father yelled directly into the phone.

"Listen, Mia," he told her. "If I made you feel sad, I'm sorry. With Judy, I mean. You're right, I didn't think about you. I guess I forgot that your kid is always your kid, even when they have kids of their own. I'm sorry."

"Grandpa!"

"It's okay, Dad," she said. "I shouldn't have been such a baby about it. I'm sorry too."

"Very good," said Ira.

The thing about Ira was that he never cared if Mia liked him. And so she liked him all the more.

The hummingbird had disappeared into the lavender sky. Mia stretched her legs in the twilight and remembered them much smaller, climbing up the ladder to the top of the playground slide. Compact toddler bodies in socks and sneakers swirled beneath her in a sea of shrieks. At the top, finally, four-year-old Mia was the king. Not a queen. A king.

All-knowing and powerful in her shorts and knee socks, different from the little girls twirling about in dresses, different from the little boys pretending to be superheroes too. Capable in a way that they were not.

On good days, when life had meaning and God existed and the soul traveled on when the body reached the end of its journey, Mia felt that she had been destined to be both a mother and a father in one. That her four-year-old self had been preparing her forty-year-old self for what was to come.

If that was true, what about her husband? Had tiny him prepared forty-four-year-old him for his fate in the same way? Was that why he had lived with such passion? The hardest part about dying were the answers that died with you.

A pair of slippers slid across the pavement of the pool deck. She turned to find Chloe approaching, wearing a giant purple-and-green tie-dyed T-shirt that skirted their knees and cheetah-spotted leggings. On their feet were two puffs of pink faux fur. They were still so young: just eleven years alive.

"Hello," said Mia.

"Hi," said Chloe. They shuffled over to the chair opposite Mia and folded themselves into it neatly. "You're an author."

"Yes."

"But you don't write kids' books."

"No. I wish I could because I like them so much, but that would require a lot of work in terms of tone and—"

"And your books have curse words in them," interrupted Chloe, a delighted smile brightening their face. "And sex."

"Sometimes they do. Because that's the way I talk. Because I'm an exhausted adult. You're a kid with lots of energy. You can find better words than—"

"Fuck," Chloe interjected.

"Well, yes, that's a good example. But I bet your parents wouldn't like to hear you say that."

"My parents don't care what I do," said Chloe. "They're always on their phones."

"Sure they do," said Mia. "But they're allowed to have their own lives too. Being a parent is a lot of work, you know."

"I won't let my mom take any pictures of me," Chloe told Mia. "I told her that if she posts anything about me on her stupid Instagram feed, I'll kill her."

"Kill?"

"That's the only time she talks to me, when she wants me to pose for some stupid picture."

"Yeah?" asked Mia, judging George and then immediately feeling guilty for doing so.

Everyone parented differently. Mia had always worked too hard at it, almost always at the expense of her own well-being. She had spent the entire first twelve months of motherhood either pumping milk from her breasts or wearing tiny plastic sombreros on her inverted nipples. She had been exhausted and drained to the point of collapse, to the point of hearing her breast pump speak to her in Hebrew, and yet she wouldn't hear of stopping. And for what? He would have been fine drinking formula. For Mia, misery was part of the parenting contract. It always had been. George, on the other hand, had no problem putting herself first. Neither was right or wrong; they just were.

"Is that what you're wearing to your reading thing?" asked Chloe now. Mia looked down at her sweatshirt and jeans.

"Oh God no. What time is it?"

Chloe looked at their phone. *They have a phone.*

Day by day, Mia reminded herself. Her older dude was eight, Chloe was eleven, Mia had three more years—

"Four o'clock," said Chloe.

Day by day.

Mia stood up suddenly, catching her sunglasses on a strand of hair. She had two hours, which was a lot of time in Mia's twenties but no time at all in her forties.

"Ow," she mumbled, disentangling them.

"What are you going to read?"

"Oh, I don't do that, that's boring. I'm going to answer some questions from your mom, and then the audience will have their turn. It's better that way. Nobody wants to hear me drone on and on."

Chloe stared at her expectantly.

"Well, bye, Chloe. It was nice talking with you."

"Mia?"

"Yeah?"

"Can I help you with your makeup and stuff?"

They were so earnest.

"Sure," said Mia. "Come on."

CHLOE HOVERED INCHES from Mia's face, not standing and not sitting, crouched in concentration. A compact of eye shadow in one small hand, a brush in the other.

"Open your eyes," they instructed Mia. Their breath smelled like cotton candy.

"I am!"

"More."

"I can't—this is as open as they will go."

"Oh." Chloe stepped back. Stood up straight. "Why are they so wrinkled?"

"I'm old," said Mia.

"My mom's eyelids aren't squishy like this."

"Well, your mom has had surgery. Right?"

"I don't know," Chloe said, and began to dab the brush in Mia's gray powder. Tentatively, they tapped the delicate skin. "Probably. She's always getting something done."

"And your dad, he does that kind of stuff for a living, right? Changes people's faces?"

"Yeah," said Chloe. "I wish I could change my face."

Mia remembered being eleven. Overnight, she had gone from liking to hating herself. Her cheeks were too big, too flushed. Her eyebrows met in the middle. And her body! Oh, how she had hated her body. It wasn't doing what her friends' bodies were doing. Instead of budding breasts, there had just been flesh. Too much flesh. Sometimes Mia would stand in front of her mirror, her door locked, and gather her stomach into both hands, willing it to flatten. She had begun to study rom-com actresses for clues on how to be desirable. She had taken this research very seriously.

> I. *Eat but never gain weight, preferably at diners*
>> A. *Cheeseburgers*
>> B. *Fries*
>> C. *Milkshakes*
> II. *Burp the alphabet*
> III. *Straighten your hair*
> IV. *Be crazy*
>> A. *Crazy is sexy*
> V. *Sex*
>> A. *Be good at it*
>> B. *But not too good*

"What's wrong with your face?" she asked Chloe now. They had moved on to Mia's bronzer, attacking her with their fluffy brush.

"It's ugly," said Chloe. "My nose is giant, and I don't have a chin."

"I love your nose," said Mia. "It's got character."

Chloe rolled their eyes. "I look like my dad."

"Your dad is—"

"Ugly."

"He's not ugly! He's handsome," Mia lied.

"Stupid Max looks just like my mom. Lucky bastard."

"Chloe! You're too young to talk like that." Mia took the brush from Chloe's hand. "Sit down," she told them.

"I know it's hard to be young. I was young once. But can I tell you something that I wish I had believed when I was your age? It would have saved me a lot of heartache."

"Fine," said Chloe. "But then I have to do your lips."

"You are only as pretty as you think you are," Mia told them. "Confidence is the key. If you walk down the street with your shoulders back and your head held high, realizing your worth, everyone else will too."

"That's not true," said Chloe.

"No, it is! Think about the popular girls in your class. Are they really pretty? Or are they just average but think they're pretty?"

Chloe considered the question. "Portland has giant ears," they told Mia.

"Portland?"

"Yeah, that's her name."

"Okay," said Mia. "But does Portland think she has giant ears?"

"She thinks she's the shit," said Chloe.

"And do the boys like her?"

"Boys and girls," said Chloe. "She was voted 'Best Looking' last year."

"You see?" said Mia. "And they have those so young?"

Chloe nodded.

"If I could go back in time and change something about myself, it wouldn't be my looks. It would be the time I wasted trying to change them. Your body is just a vessel. Might as well be kind to it."

"So you're saying that I'm not pretty," said Chloe. They rooted in Mia's makeup bag and pulled out a lipstick.

"Chloe! That's not what I'm saying at all."

Chloe smiled. "I know," they said. "I get what you're saying, I guess. But my mom doesn't."

"What do you mean?"

Chloe slid the lipstick across Mia's mouth. "You should tell her what you just told me. She doesn't like herself at all."

"Why do you say that?"

"Don't move your mouth!"

"She doesn't like aging, but she likes herself."

"Do you like aging?" Chloe stood back and admired their work.

"It's better than dying," Mia told them.

"I LIKE THIS bohemian-chef vibe thing you have going," George offered from the driver's seat, pointing to Mia's beige jumpsuit. Black geometric shapes floated across its heavy linen fabric.

"I'm not a chef."

Mia's phone dinged, the sound of an incoming text. Her publicist.

Hello! Hope California is a dream. The reading is still on tonight, but Ellen the owner has asked that you wear a mask. She'll have one for you and all of the attendees at the register. Knock 'em dead!

Mia hadn't read the news in a very long time because it put her in a markedly worse mood. She had heard rumors of a virus in China, she didn't live under a rock, but she hadn't gotten much further than that.

We're wearing masks now? This is real? she typed.

Opaque bubbles danced on Mia's screen.

Oh, it's real all right. They're talking about shutting down the whole country.

Mia's stomach turned. She was however many—she didn't know, geography had never been her strong suit, but it was a lot—miles away from the dudes. This did not bode well.

I have a cousin in Korea who's been in lockdown for months.

So now not only had her mother and her husband died, but now she was capping the decade with a pandemic? This was really happening? Mia put the phone down and gazed out the window. Of course it was happening. Why wouldn't it be happening?

"Hey, George, what do you know about this Covid thing?" Mia asked, turning back to her.

"Is it Covid, or is it Corona? Like it's not terrifying enough, it has to have two names?" George shook her head. "I dunno. There's a cruise ship full of it out there in the Pacific somewhere, apparently." She gestured toward the window. "It's set to dock here, like, any day."

"Oh my God," said Mia. "Am I stuck here?"

"You could do worse," said George.

Great, thought Mia, staring out the window as they coasted down a giant hill, the lights of the city twinkling all around them. Now she had to Joan of Arc her way across a continent too? When did it fucking end?

"Should we just bypass the reading and go straight to the airport?" she asked, half-serious.

She had told the dudes that she wouldn't die on this trip. She had to make good on that.

Day by day really didn't apply to a pandemic, Mia thought, her heart racing. But it had to. It had to.

"Mia, calm down," said George. "I'm sure it's just like the flu or something. The media is always hysterical. That's their job." She reached into her bag and pulled out a pill bottle. "Here, take a Valium."

"No, I'm good," said Mia. "Those things knock me out."

"Suit yourself," George said, and placed one on her tongue. "Oh look, there's the bookstore!"

"Actually, maybe I will take one." George deposited a tiny white circle in the palm of Mia's hand as she parallel parked.

"George, what are you going to do about Todd?" Mia asked her after she swallowed the pill whole. "You can't keep living like this. Chloe's a smart kid. She knows what's going on. I mean they. They know what's going on."

"Why, did they say something?"

"No," Mia lied. "But they're perceptive."

George turned off the car and faced Mia.

"I've set things up to the best of my ability, Mia. Let the cards fall where they may. I'm not like you. I don't have a job that I'm passionate about. I'm passionate about my lifestyle, which I know is less than you want from me, but it is what it is."

"You know that I hate that phrase," said Mia. "You did that on purpose."

"Maybe."

"What does it even mean? 'It is what it is'? I can't. And what about Chloe?" asked Mia.

"They're almost a teenager, Mia. They're going to hate me no matter what."

"I don't think they feel seen by you."

"Oh, I see them all right. Those slippers!" George winced.

"George, I mean it. They need you, even if they're pushing you away."

"Fine. I'll take them to lunch once a week so they can ignore me over sushi."

"Okay," agreed Mia. "But don't post about it!"

"Fine."

Everything would be all right as long as there were books to read, thought Mia as she climbed out of George's car. Right? As long as the human experience was rendered on the page, as long as people saw themselves in other people's experiences.

Mia's mother had begun taking Mia to the library when she was tiny, so tiny that one of her first memories was grabbing the hand of a woman who she thought was her mother, only to real-ize with terror that it wasn't her at all. Whether Mia's mother had passed her love of words to Mia by practice or genetics or both, Mia didn't know, but she was so grateful. Words were her job. She got paid, albeit not enough, to hang out with words.

"You're in the window!" George exclaimed, pointing to Mia's author photo staring back at them. It was like staring at a distant cousin, Mia realized. One without circles under her eyes and a halo of frizz around her head.

"Quick, let's get a photo!" said George, pushing her toward it.

"No, George, really, I—"

"Shut up and pose," said George. "Honestly, Mia, these books aren't going to sell themselves. You have to post. Give me your phone."

Mia smiled half-heartedly while George directed her: *Pop your knee! Put your hand on your hip! Look happy!* She knew she would pore over the photos later in bed, berating herself for looking old, or fat, or old and fat, and she was bored by herself already. But maybe this time she wouldn't. Maybe she was done wasting her own time.

"No, George, stop," she told her. "I can't have the last photo on my phone be of myself."

"What do you mean, 'the last photo'?"

"Covid? The apocalypse?"

"Are you trying to be funny?" asked George.

"Laughing through the tears, maybe? I don't know what to think. It's like, things are so incredibly bad across the board, and now we have a raging virus killing people left and right? People are in lockdowns inside their homes? What does that even mean? What is the future going to look like?"

"It's not looking good, I'll tell you that," said George.

"What the fuck?" Mia shook her head. The concept of being stuck in her house with the dudes for the rest of their lives had only been metaphorical thus far. The idea that it could become literal in a matter of weeks or days sent a chill down her spine. Was it really going to be that bad?

"I know," said George. "I can see what's coming, but I also can't see it because I don't want to, if that makes sense? Anyway. Let's go back to talking about photos. What is the last photo on your phone?" George scrolled through. "Is this a bag of chips?"

"I wanted to remember to try them."

"That's how you want to be remembered?" asked George, following Mia through the bookshop door. "As a chip enthusiast? You don't even eat chips."

The shop smelled like books: a hint of cedar, a touch of sweat, and a dash of tobacco, the last being Mia's favorite smell. Colorful jackets climbed up the walls and crowded the shelves like postage stamps.

Mia's phone rang.

"Hi!" Mia's younger son squeaked from the screen. He had the voice of a mob boss.

"Hi, buddy, how are you?" she asked. "What are you doing up?"

Her elder grabbed the phone. "Hi!" he declared.

"Give it back!" her younger screeched.

"Share the phone, please," she commanded. "Or I'm hanging up."

The screen cleared, and both of them stared back at her from the couch, their clear eyes wide and sparkling, their lashes impossibly long, and their cheeks as round and glossy as apples.

"You look beautiful," her younger declared shyly.

"It's true," said her elder. "Say thank you."

"Thank you," said Mia.

"Move back!" her elder said to his brother.

"No, you move back!"

"Guys."

The screen steadied. Now Mia was looking at the wall.

"Turn the phone around, please, so I can see both of your handsome faces.

"Hi," she said to two pairs of eyes: one brown and the other blue. "I really miss you."

"We miss you too," they sang.

"How's it going with Grandpa?" she asked them.

"You have makeup on!" her younger barked accusingly.

"Yes, I have a book party tonight," she explained.

"Another one?"

"Yes, another one."

"She's famous, remember?" her older one said to his brother.

"Oh yeah," he said. "Will there be shrimps at this party?"

"No," said Mia. "No shrimp."

"Oh," he said.

"Is Grandpa around?" asked Mia. "I'd love to talk to him."

"Yeah." The phone began to move, and Mia was privy to a personal viewing of the inside of her elder son's nostrils.

"Grandpa!" he yelled. "Grandpa! My mom is on the phone!"

The screen whizzed past the kitchen cabinets, around the refrigerator, and then out the back door and into the yard.

"Your mom? That's my daughter you're talking about," she heard Ira say as the phone made its way to him.

"You again?" he asked. Snow dusted the branches of the two evergreen trees behind him. "Where are you now? Your party? Let me see what you're wearing." Mia held the phone out so he could see.

"Pretty as a picture and smart as a whip," he told her.

"Your yard looks like that show, about the chemist?" She could see it behind him—littered with mounds of snirt, the trees bare, the bushes spindly. A headless baby doll peeked out of the overgrown kudzu.

"*Breaking Bad*?"

"Yeah, that's the one."

"Listen, guys, I have to go do my thing now," said Mia. "I love you. And go to bed already!"

"We love you too!" the dudes chorused, and then immediately began to wrestle shoeless and shirtless in the frigid air.

"Hey, guys, give me a break!" her dad yelled at them. "Get in the house and put on some clothes, for God's sake. Now!"

"Hey, Dad, before you go—what's the word on the street with this Covid mishigas?" Mia asked.

"I wouldn't call it mishigas," he answered. "I'm hearing that their school is gonna shut down."

"What?"

Mia's stomach bottomed out. She searched the store for a

bathroom. Some people needed to know where the emergency exit was; Mia needed to know where the bathroom was.

"Yeah, that's what the Oriental mom at the park was saying."

"Chinese, Dad, Jesus fucking Christ, are you serious? 'Oriental'?"

"What is this, the U.N.? Excuse me, Chinese."

"Fuuuuuuuuck," Mia said on a giant exhale. "They're really talking about closing?"

"Mia Macher?" said a voice, a nervous voice. Mia looked up to see a pleasantly plump woman ensconced in head-to-toe aubergine velvet standing before her.

"Let's not worry until we have to worry, okay?" Ira said. "Deal?"

"Deal," said Mia. "But let me know the second we have to worry."

"And stop calling, it's enough already. Go enjoy yourself, we're fine."

"They called me!" she argued as the screen went blank.

"Sorry," she offered to the woman in velvet. "My kids. I'm Mia. Thank you so much for having me."

"I'm Ellen, and it's a pleasure," she replied from behind a blue surgical mask. In her top and pants, which draped from her collarbone to the tips of her round-toed black flats, she looked like she was melting.

"I just loved your book—so real and so raw. I lost my son when he was twenty-four from a drug overdose, so I know your pain," she offered. "Well, not your pain specifically, my husband was a piece of shit and we divorced right after our daughter was born, but the loss of a loved one, a loss that shatters your heart into a million pieces, I know what that's like."

Mia moved to hug her, but Ellen threw up her hands defensively.

"I'm sorry, but I can't hug." She pointed to her mask. "Covid. I have masks for you two as well, if you don't mind." They dangled from her hand.

"Oh," said Mia. "Right, of course." She looped one over her ears and felt immediately ridiculous.

"I thought they said we don't have to wear masks?" asked George, frowning. "Didn't the C.D.C. just say that? This is going to ruin my makeup."

"Well, that just doesn't make any sense now, does it?" Ellen told them angrily. "Not wearing a mask in a pandemic is dumb, although I'd expect nothing less with this president at the helm. Do yourselves a favor and don't listen to anyone but Fauci."

"Who's Fauci?" asked Mia, feeling dumb.

"The chief medical advisor to the president?" Ellen's gaze confirmed Mia's fears. She was dumb. Willfully dumb, anyway. "He says wear a mask."

"Okay," Mia said, and put hers on.

"So where are the people?" asked George as she adjusted hers over her nose.

"We have thirteen readers in the back room," said Ellen. "And they're all masked. Honestly, I'm shocked anyone showed up at all."

"Oh," said Mia.

"No, no, not because of you, dear."

"People are risking death to see you!" exclaimed George. "That's a tweet."

"Oh boy," said Mia. "This is a first."

One thing Mia had done right in her career was taken her ego and tossed it into a landfill when she'd begun. There were going to be good reviews, and there were going to be very bad reviews. There were going to be days when her fingers danced over the keyboard as though possessed, and there were going to be days when she squeezed out two sentences in three hours. Mia had done readings where no one had showed, and she had done readings where actual fans showed up. It was always a crapshoot.

"Shall we?" Ellen asked, and led them to a makeshift stage in the back of her store. It faced an audience of metal folding chairs on which the promised thirteen guests sat.

"Do you have wine?" asked Mia as they turned to greet her. Seeing them with their masks on, Mia felt like she was going to be operated on.

"We do," said Ellen.

WHEN MIA WAS a teenager, her parents had been disgusted by what they called her lack of authenticity. How could she be so nasty to them but so nice to her friends?

"You're fake," Ira would tell her, his blue eyes hurt and confused. "I hate fake people."

"I'm not fake!" Mia would scream back before running to her room and slamming the door. But she knew that sometimes she pretended to be happy when she wasn't. That she made jokes when she was sad. That she was polite to people she disliked.

Was she less of a person because she wasn't always the same person? she had wondered, lying on her quilt-covered bed and staring at the ceiling, her face wet with tears.

Why she felt so compelled to please people, or at least stimulate them at all costs, wasn't clear to Mia, but she had liked this about herself less and less with age.

She had discovered that by being anyone she wanted to be on the page, she could be herself, for better or worse, in real life.

A woman in the front row wearing a purple beret raised her hand. "I'm so sorry for your loss," she told Mia.

"I appreciate that. Thank you."

"I'm a widow too, but I would never write about my husband like you did, without his permission."

"What?" Mia asked.

"What would he say about you writing about him like he's dead?"

"He is dead."

"But for you to capitalize on it, I don't think it's right." Purple Beret looked at Mia expectantly.

"Mia?" asked George.

Mia looked at George, her eyes wide. Who was this awful woman in this awful hat?

"She asked you how long it took you to write your memoir," nudged George.

"She did?" What was happening? The inside of Mia's mouth felt like sandpaper. She took a sip of her water.

"Did this take longer to write than your others?" asked George.

Are you okay? George asked her with her eyes.

"Um, yes, this did take longer to write," said Mia.

I'm not okay, Mia answered silently.

"Thank you," Purple Beret said, and sat down.

"I'm sorry, would you mind if we took a bathroom break?" George asked Ellen.

"By all means, go right ahead." The masked crowd shifted in their seats, sensing something was wrong but not knowing what exactly.

In the tiny bathroom, Mia collapsed onto the toilet lid, narrowly avoiding a stack of books piled up next to it.

"What's going on?" asked George.

"I heard her ask me an entirely different question," said Mia. "I heard her ask me what it felt like to capitalize on his death."

"Whoa," said George. "Do you need smelling salts or something? Lip gloss?" She checked her own in the mirror. George had never been able to pass a mirror without looking into it.

"Why did I hear that?"

"I don't know," said George. "Have you ever combined Valium and wine before? Some people claim it's a bad combination, but I swear by it."

"I guess I haven't," said Mia, thinking. "And I guess I won't be doing it again. Jesus. I was fully having a schizophrenic episode back there."

"Lightweight," said George. "*Do* you think you're capitalizing on his death?"

"No," answered Mia. "Well, maybe. But that wasn't my intention!"

"Take it easy," said George. "*I* know that. Do *you* know that?"

"It was the only way I could process it. The only way I could keep going. The only way I could immortalize the happiest years of my life. With him."

"Okay," said George. "That's how I see it too. That's how anyone with a heart sees it."

"There was no other way. Not for me."

Mia drank her water. Every time she wrote a book, her insecurities rose up from the murk of her subconscious, like her own Loch Ness Monster. *I'm not a good writer; this is boring; who cares; what's the point?*

But her other books had been novels. A memoir was a different beast. She wasn't just judging her skill; she was judging herself. The bad reviews she had read echoed her most private and most hurtful thoughts. Why had she done this to herself, after all that she had been through?

"Listen, Mia, you had to write this. To move past it."

"No, not to move past it, George. To move through it. My memories are all I have. They're all the dudes have. They don't even remember him! Do you know how sad that makes me?" Mia started to cry.

"Everything okay in there?" asked Ellen from the other side of the door.

"Oh yes, just some diarrhea!" called George.

"We'll be right out! Shit. My mascara." She stood up and faced the tin mirror.

"Here," George said, and handed her a square of toilet paper. "Listen, Mia, you did what you had to do and ended up with a love letter to your husband. It's a triumph, what you did, even if

it doesn't sell the way you wish it would sell. Why are you so hard
on yourself?"

"It's the way I was raised, I guess." Mia dabbed at her under-
eyes and then blew her nose.

"You can't care what other people think, Mia. We're too old for
that shit."

"That's rich, coming from someone who's botoxed within an
inch of her life."

"Mia! That's mean. And anyway, this"—she pointed to herself—
"is for me. Just because my life is a mess doesn't mean I have to
look a mess. I don't care what other people think, you dum-dum.
I care what I think. And I think I look good."

"You do look good," said Mia. "Really good. I'm sorry I said that.
It's just, the chasm between what we put out in the world versus
how we feel on the inside is so big sometimes. It's too much."

"But you bridged that gap with your memoir. You put your vulnerability on display for everyone to read. That's a good thing.
That's inspiring. He would be proud of you."

"He would?"

"Yes."

Mia was her own worst critic, but she wrote anyway. Because
she didn't know what else to do with all the voices in her head—
the bad and the good. The only way she could quiet them was to
put them on the page.

"Now let's go back out. Ellen is probably having a heart attack."

MIA AND GEORGE sat outside a fancy bar at which a glass of wine
cost sixteen dollars, pondering the near disaster of Mia's reading.

Had the voice she'd heard been the Valium and the wine talking? Maybe. Had it been her mother's voice chiding her? Also maybe. Was Mia her own worst enemy? Ultimately it didn't matter. Mia had done the best she could with the cards she'd been dealt.

Do your best and fuck the rest, she always told the dudes. She missed them: their incessant needs, their constant bothering, their warm and solid snuggles. She was teaching them to be the best versions of themselves because that was what she'd been taught. They had different deliveries, Mia and her parents, but the message was the same.

"Oh man," said Mia to George. "Am I going to make it back before the world ends?"

The universe seemed to be teetering on the brink of extinction, and yet Mia sat in San Francisco, drinking wine and indulging her ego while her sons ate Ira's fruit surprise three thousand miles away. She had googled the distance on her phone and now she knew.

"I think so," said George. "But I'm not one hundred percent sure."

"Well, that's how I feel about everything, so?" Mia shrugged. "Maybe I should cut my trip short and go home."

"What else is on tap? Chicago and Atlanta?"

Mia nodded.

"How many more days?"

"Four."

"I really don't know what you should do," said George.

"I'm all they have, you know. I can't die."

"But you will. Someday."

"Thanks." Mia smiled weakly.

Maybe she could look into changing her flight. But if the rumors were true, if they were going into lockdown, she might never be able to leave the dudes again. No girls' trips on the horizon. No book tours. No visits. No help.

No help.

Day by day.

"You know, all the pictures I post, of my so-called happy life with my perfect kids and perfect husband?"

"Yes," said Mia.

"I wait and I wait for someone to call me out, but it never happens. It's like I'm begging someone to really see me, but nobody ever does. Except you." George sighed. "Thank you for that."

"Well, what would happen if you posted something real?"

"Oh God, no one wants to see that."

"How do you know?" asked Mia. "Holding the mirror up makes me feel less lonely."

"Yeah, but no one needs another selfie of a rich white lady crying."

"Fair," said Mia. "But it doesn't have to be that literal, you know."

"Excuse me?" A woman in a sparkly jumpsuit stood beside Mia and George at the bar.

"Yes?" George said.

"Would you mind taking our picture?"

"Sure, of course," Mia said, and stood up to take the woman's camera.

She motioned to her friends to join her, one of whom was draped in a sash. *Bride,* it read in pink bedazzled letters.

"Oh, you're getting married!" said George.

"Yep," they answered.

"Is she the first of you?" asked Mia as she clicked away. "Put your hands on your hips. That's good." *Click, click, click.* Pictures were all she had left of her husband. Mia understood their importance.

"I am," said the bride. "Are you guys married?"

Mia looked at George.

"I am," said George.

"Any advice?" she asked.

"Whatever you don't like about him is not going to change," said George. "If you can accept that, by all means, get married. If you can't, maybe don't."

"Geez," said the bride.

"You asked," said George.

"What about you?" another of the women asked Mia.

"Just enjoy it," said Mia.

"Okay," said the bride. "Thanks." She took the phone back from Mia and the women galloped away.

"Because one of you is going to die!" Mia screamed after them.

"This is who we are now," offered George, nodding.

"Take it or leave it," said Mia.

"Look at us," said George, sitting back down and motioning to the waiter. "I'm trying to take my husband for all he's worth, and yours is dead. What happened to us?"

"Life," said Mia. "And death."

"Were your parents happy?" George asked. "Growing up?"

"Not really. I never saw them touch each other. And they yelled a lot."

"Same," said George. "Although they gave each other the silent treatment instead. Wasps don't yell."

"And they stayed together," said Mia. "Why?"

"Money," answered George. "The more things change, I guess."

"When my mom got sick, everything changed," Mia told George. "My father took care of her. I'd never seen him be tender before. It was beautiful, actually."

"That's nice. I guess that's why people stay together, then. Money and hospice care. Selena can change my bedpan."

"George," said Mia. "What are you going to do when your plan works? Isn't your heart going to break? To see him with someone else?"

"That's the point: I never see him," said George. "We live totally separate lives. Even if they do get together, it won't be on my watch."

"God, it's just so depressing, George," said Mia. "Do you even know how much money you have in the bank? Maybe you don't have to bait him with Selena, you know? Is your name on the mortgage?"

"I don't know," said George.

"How can you not know?"

"I don't want to know," said George.

"That's just dumb. This is the kind of stuff you need to know, especially if you want to divide it down the road. It's empowering to know what you have. Then you don't have to rely on Todd the way you do."

"Mia, who are you, Suze Orman? You never knew about this stuff either until you had to."

"True," said Mia. "But I'm so glad that I do. Not being involved in your finances is like cavewoman shit, George. It's 2020. Didn't you read my memoir?"

George was quiet.

"You didn't read it, did you?"

"Mia, you know I don't like to read. And anyway, I lived it. I don't need to read it."

They sat in silence, nursing wounds that hadn't yet healed. Mia's attempt to save George wasn't working, but maybe that was because she was still in the process of saving herself.

"Where do you think you would be if he hadn't died?" asked George finally. "Do you think you would be happy?"

"I don't know. I'd like to think that whatever problems came up, we would have handled them. Together. Although I guess I'll never know."

"I think you're right," said George. She reached across the table and took Mia's hand. "You two were really in love. You could feel it."

"You could?" asked Mia.

"Yeah."

Tears of relief rolled down Mia's cheeks. "Thank you, George."

"You're welcome," she whispered, crying too.

"Hey, girls," said Todd, wandering into the kitchen after Mia and George had returned. "How was your thing?" he asked Mia.

"Good," answered George, not looking up.

"What kinds of books do you write again?" Todd asked Mia. "Chick lit, right?"

Mia bristled, all her arm hairs standing on end.

"It's not chick lit," she told him. "It's fiction. Fiction featuring female protagonists."

"Oh, so chick lit superheroes," Todd said, and laughed a hearty, patronizing laugh.

"And what do you do?" Mia asked him. "You suck eyelid wrinkles off middle-aged women with a vacuum all day, right?"

Todd stopped laughing. George peered down at her chest, a smile across her lips.

"Jesus, relax, Mia," said Todd. "I guess you can't take a joke."

"No. I can take a joke if it's, you know, funny."

Mia stood up and walked through the massive French doors, across the deck, down the stairs, past the saltwater pool, through the yard with its rectangular plots of curated wildflowers, and into her two-story, two-bedroom-and-two-bath guest home to an L-shaped couch, where she finally collapsed.

Anger was new to Mia. Her parents had yelled for sport, but she had made the decision not to be that way because it didn't work. Her parents had never solved anything with anger.

Mia would hide from the dudes whenever a surge overtook her, cursing in jagged whispers in her locked bathroom until her anger went away. But was it good to hide those feelings? Was she teaching them to be ashamed of rage instead of how to channel it properly? Was there a proper way to channel rage, even?

She sat up on the couch and rubbed her eyes. Why did Todd get to live? He was a terrible person.

There was a soft knock at the door.

"I'm sorry about Todd," George said. She had taken off her stilettos and looked small enough to break.

"Remember David's Bagels?" Mia asked.

"Oh, we're talking about that? Everything with butter. Toasted."

"Toasted pumpernickel with veggie cream cheese and a slice of tomato but only if—"

"The tomatoes looked right," finished George.

For three years, they had taken turns for their Saturday-morning bagel runs, dutifully ordering for two and returning to an apartment that smelled of weed and sandalwood to unwrap and rehash the events of the night before.

"Do you remember Camp Time?" asked George, smiling. It was so good to see her smiling—smiling-with-her-eyes smiling—and Mia wanted more.

"That was the best."

"You would be in your bed and I would be in my bed and we would talk each other to sleep."

"Like two turtledoves," said Mia.

"And do you remember the thing you used to always do? When you would make up a happily-ever-after story for me?" asked George.

"Of course. And then I would try to force you to return the favor, but you never did."

"I'm not a storyteller," said George.

"Who was that British mortgage broker guy? Sam?" asked Mia.

"Geoff."

"Ah yes, Geoff with a 'G,'" said Mia.

"George and Geoff, remember?"

"Gross," said Mia. "George, you have the worst taste in men."

"I know," said George. "And my dad's a nice guy, so I don't get it."

Mia nodded, even though George's dad was not a nice guy at all. "If you lost ten pounds, you would be a knockout," he had told Mia once.

"You always knew that you wanted to be a writer," said George. "That was the first thing you said to me."

"But I wrote nothing when we were living together."

"Yeah, but still. You talked about wanting to do it. And then you freaking did it. Do you know how amazing that is?"

"Sometimes," said Mia.

"Well, I never had a goal like that."

"Acting!" Mia insisted.

"No, that was just one of my phases. You have the drive of a Mack truck."

Mia grabbed George's hand and pulled her down next to her. Sometimes lately, Mia had begun to suspect that she might be a badass, and it both delighted and frightened her to have her suspicion confirmed.

"I love you," she told George.

"I know," said George.

CHAPTER 10

Mia marveled at the efficiency of the El train even as her shoulder throbbed and her neck muscles screamed. Any time Mia sat down, her exhaustion sat with her.

Chicago whizzed by her window. After a disconcerting flight plagued by masked zombies, she was embarking on the second half of her journey, to Rachel. For all Mia knew, this would be the last time she could leave her house. She would finish what she started. Mia had seen on the airport televisions, as she hunched over a cup of six-dollar coffee, that people were maniacally Cloroxing their vegetables now. Mia would not be Cloroxing her vegetables. Death was coming for whom it was coming for, no matter what. She'd seen it firsthand, twice over. That said, she would certainly wear a mask and scour her hands. She didn't want to die because she was an idiot.

Rachel had asked Mia if she wanted to be picked up at the airport, but Mia wanted to take the El. It reminded her of the New York subway, and the subway reminded her of her husband. She had met him on the subway, which sounded made up but wasn't.

She looked at the damp Post-it in her hand, on which the names of three train stations were scrawled, and then she looked at the map on the wall.

She had time. Time to remember. She leaned against the window and then thought better of it and sat up straight.

The morning she had met her husband, he was standing on the grafittied train platform in the Brooklyn spring air, his dark hair damp. For four years Mia had been seeing him on the train; for four years he had been her "subway crush," and for four years she had never gotten up the nerve to say hello to him.

But on that day, she decided to do it.

It would either go right or horribly wrong, but if it was the latter, she would just have to change subway lines, which was annoying but not the end of the world.

A train had pulled in as Mia descended the last of the stairs, and out of habit, she had jumped on, just in time to realize that her subway crush had not. And then, there he was again, gliding through the gap just as the doors reopened, and with two friends in tow.

Two friends she knew! She had felt lucky that day, for the first time in her life.

Her hands had been trembling when she told him.

"I see you on the train all the time!"

Her voice had shaken.

"I see you too!" he had replied, in a voice that was not at all the voice that she had imagined. A kind voice.

God, that moment. Mia replayed it in her mind as often as she could. She had known in her heart, as she walked down Sixth Avenue in the spring air afterward, that Subway Crush would be her husband. It sounded nuts—it had felt nuts to her at the time—but she had felt it nonetheless. And she had been right.

The El chugged into Mia's station, the second one on her Post-it list. She placed her tote bag on top of her suitcase and stood, bracing for the cold.

Was she supposed to wait here on this freezing platform for her next train? She glanced up, read the sign, and checked her Post-it again.

Yes.

But if she had been as right as she knew she'd been about him, what did that mean for what had happened? Had she been supposed to write him back into existence all along? Was that why she was missing from her memoir? She had the rest of her life to live. All he had was the page. And so she had given it to him.

Mia's phone rang, and she dug in the pocket of her coat to find it. Her hand felt like a shark fin. Why was it so fucking cold here?

"Hey, guys," Mia said, her teeth chattering.

"Mom! Mom!" they cried, and Mia battled the dueling forces of love and irritation that defined her motherhood.

"Guys, chill out. You can each hold the phone for two minutes. Set the timer." Her elder handed it to his brother, conceding to the proposed plan.

"So, Mom," her younger said. "I had a dream!" he declared, positioning the phone perpendicularly to his mouth like the walkietalkies Mia had lost on purpose.

"Oh, cool. What happened in your dream?"

"So," he said, settling against the navy micro-suede cushions of their couch. "We survived an obstacle course."

"Oh!" said Mia.

"The first level had smashers with spikes on the end."

"Oh my goodness!" said Mia. "Spikes!"

"And then in the second level, guess what?"

"What?"

"Pennywise tried to eat us, and he ate our cheeks, and we were bleeding!"

"Our cheeks!"

"And then in the third level, there was a tiger, and there was blood coming out of his teeth and we went under his toes and we won the whole thing."

"Under his toes?"

"But then we dropped to the floor," he finished solemnly.

"And then what?" asked Mia.

"That's the end," he told her.

"Mom, it's been way more than two minutes," her elder informed her as he crowded the frame, his brown eyes flashing.

"Yes, you're right. Sorry. Go ahead."

"So you know how Squiggly hasn't been eating and we thought he was probably going to die?"

"Yeah." Squiggly was their moody Betta fish.

"So guess what?"

"What?"

"He usually eats at five but last night we forgot because we were watching the news with Grandpa and so I didn't feed him until seven!"

"Oh no," said Mia, worrying more about their watching the news than Squiggly.

"And when I came up to his bowl, he was actually begging for food!"

"He was? How does a fish beg?"

"Well, he was flipping his arms at me," he explained.

Squiggly was bloodred. When the light caught him just right, he looked like a wet Valentine.

"Oh," said Mia.

"And then he ate! Like really ate!"

"That's great!" said Mia.

"So that means that you'll make it back here okay, and you won't get the coronavirus," he reasoned.

"Mmm," said Mia. "How so?"

"Well, we thought he would die, but he didn't. So it's a sign. We thought you might die coming back, but now we know that you won't!"

"You thought I was going to die?" asked Mia, her heart sinking. "I thought we went over that."

"I dunno. Maybe. The coronavirus is killing everybody. You can get it from the grocery store, you know."

"I really don't think I'm going to die right now," she told him, because she didn't. "And I'm being very careful. Please don't worry about me, honey. I'm not your responsibility. I'm your mom."

"Well, I don't have to anyway. I saw the sign."

He was always seeing signs—a butterfly in the backyard when he mentioned his father's name, a double rainbow on his birthday. She had only seen that kind of optimism once before in her life, from his father.

Her train pulled in, and she waddled aboard, balancing the

phone on her shoulder with her chin. Her frozen body no longer felt like her body; it felt more like an idea of a body.

"Okay, honey," she told him. "I'm glad you feel better about things."

These dudes. It wasn't fair that they knew death so personally. *Day by day.*

"Hey, is Grandpa around?" she asked. *SportsCenter* blared in the background: the telltale sign.

"Hi, dear," he said, taking the phone. He looked tired, peering over his glasses at Mia.

"Sorry, they called me."

"No, it's okay. It's good to see you, I have a question. Here, let me get up." The phone rocked back and forth as he exhumed himself from the couch. "Boys, turn on one of your shows."

"So, Mia, their school is closed," he told her from the kitchen.

"What?"

"Yeah, they closed up. Sent 'em home with their computers."

"Are you okay?"

"Yeah, I'm okay. What else do I have to do? I'm here, why not?"

"Do they have schedules?"

"Yeah, but I'm going rogue."

"Dad!"

"Mia, gimme a break, will you? I'm homeschooling two gorillas here."

"Okay, Dad, whatever you need. You're right. Do you need me to come home? Because I will."

"No, enjoy yourself."

"But, Dad, aren't you exhausted? What about your naps?" Her father took two naps a day and wondered why he couldn't sleep at night.

"I'm sleeping here the best I've ever slept in my life. Don't worry about my naps."

"Okay," said Mia. "I won't worry about your naps. Dad?"

"Yeah?"

"How come you told me that the Machers didn't have any luck?"

"What?"

"When I was little, you told me that. That I wasn't a lucky person by blood."

"No, I didn't."

"Dad, you did!"

"Wasn't me."

"Dad!"

"I didn't say that, but it happens to be true. That's why your success is so meaningful."

"But I've felt lucky in my life, Dad. It's just not true what you said."

"Is it luck, or is it timing?" he asked.

"What's the difference?"

"Luck is one-dimensional. Timing requires work."

"Oh," said Mia.

He was right. Damnit, he was always right.

But perception was subjective; that was the essence of writing. Maybe he hadn't said it at all; maybe he was right. But Mia had heard it.

Her husband would tell her later, on their first date, that she had been his subway crush too. That he had wanted to say hello but that she had always avoided his gaze. Nothing could have been further from the truth.

Everyone's truth was different. The trick was accepting that.

CHAPTER 11

Mia stared up at Rachel's squat three-story apartment building. A hair salon occupied its bottom floor with plant-filled windows. The higher floors housed residents, of which Rachel and her husband, Mitch, were two. Mia rolled through the cherry-red door and buzzed their apartment.

"Hi!" cooed Rachel as she opened the door.

"Hi!" They stood awkwardly, looking at each other.

"I'm not sure it's safe to hug?" Rachel asked.

"But I can come in, right?"

"Of course, of course! Sorry."

Rachel pulled the door back, trapping herself against a wall of closets in the process.

"Is Mitch home?" asked Mia, falling onto her couch.

"He's always home," said Rachel.

"Oh," said Mia.

"Yeah," said Rachel.

"You okay?" asked Mia.

"I guess," answered Rachel.

Rachel was not one to dissect her feelings as they happened. She was more of a wait-and-see kind of person. This did not always work out for her, but sometimes it did. Mia had seen both results in real time at very different stages of their lives.

"You want to talk about it?" asked Mia now.

"Not when he's right here," said Rachel quietly. "Later. Are you okay? You look mad."

"I'm frozen solid," Mia explained.

"Don't be such a wuss!" Rachel ribbed as Mitch's footsteps made their way down the short hall toward them.

"Hi, Mitch!"

"Hey, Mia," he answered, grinning. His teeth twinkled in his dense salt-and-pepper beard like Christmas tree lights.

"Rachel says we can't hug," she told him.

"What a dud. What can I get you?" he asked.

"Any kind of alcohol that will melt me."

"Coming up."

Mia looked at his broad back, the way his shoulder blades moved underneath his sweatshirt, and wondered, Was an unemployed husband really that bad?

"He needs a purpose other than the perfect piecrust, okay, Mia?" Rachel had told her. "Like, my libido is nonexistent enough. Now my husband wears an apron all day and plays *Minecraft*? No thank you."

"Are you writing anything, Mitch?" Mia asked him now.

"God I wish," he said, and padded over to her in his leather-soled wool socks.

Mia had given her husband a pair of those once. Footage of the exchange began to roll in her mind: the sweatpants she had been wearing, the plaid flannel that had made him look like Paddington.

"I haven't been able to write in months," Mitch continued.

"Oh no, I'm sorry," said Mia.

"My brain is—" Mitch stuck his tongue out and crossed his eyes to demonstrate its uselessness.

"I know that feeling," said Mia. Rachel was pretending to sleep in an orange chair.

"Are you warming up at all?" asked Mitch.

"Yes," she answered, and took a sip of her drink. It burned her esophagus, and Mia thought of her aunt, who had almost overdosed on Rolaids once. She had gone to the emergency room and everything.

"Hey, Mia," Mitch blurted out excitedly, "you wanna smoke a joint?"

"Okay." She had nothing to do, nowhere to be. Why not? She tugged at her hat to remove it.

"But not in here," said Mitch. "Outside."

"You want me to go back into that tundra for a joint?"

"It's really good stuff."

"Fine," Mia said, and followed him out the door. "Rachel?"

"I'm good," she answered, her eyes still closed.

Outside, she and Mitch hid in an alleyway.

"You still smoke joints?" asked Mia as he lit it.

"Of course, man. Gummies are for pussies."

Mia wrinkled her nose.

"Sorry, sorry!" said Mitch. "I know I can't say that anymore. Gummies are for shafts?"

"Eh," said Mia.

Rachel had brought Mitch to a house party in Fort Greene back when Mitch was just a guy she was dating and people had parties. Mia had liked him right away. He was funny, he was kind, he was cute, he was Jewish. What was not to like?

Mitch passed the joint to her.

"Man, I haven't smoked weed in a long time," she announced, feeling wary about the high it promised. What did weed do to grief? She would find out, she guessed.

"I see that," said Mitch, taking it from her as she coughed. "Are you okay?"

"I'm fine," Mia said finally as he patted her on the back with one hand and smoked with the other. "God, how embarrassing."

"Don't be embarrassed, it's just me: a middle-aged, out-of-work comedy writer. No judgment."

Mia raised her eyebrow at him.

"Well, maybe a little."

She snatched the joint back from him and took another puff. Once upon a time in college, Mia had smoked weed every day. Maybe she would take it up again.

"How are the dudes?" he asked her.

"Good," she told him. "I know it sounds corny, but they really do make me a better person."

"That doesn't sound corny," said Mitch.

"You never wanted kids?" she asked Mitch.

"I wouldn't say that I absolutely, no way, no how didn't want to have kids, but I wasn't eager to. I just didn't see the point. They never seem to do anything but stress their parents out and then resent them, you know?" Mitch took a hit and exhaled a dragon-size plume of smoke.

"I know," agreed Mia. "I guess you have to want that stress, at least in a small way, or find it familiar, at least."

"Yeah. That sounds right." Mitch sighed loudly, and Mia felt his sadness as though it were her own.

"Rachel won't let you smoke inside?" she asked him. "Ever?"

"Never."

"When did she start cracking down?"

"About eight months ago. Unemployment has been, shall we say, challenging for us? This helps."

"Oh," said Mia, as if she hadn't heard all this before.

"I feel like she hates me," he told Mia, taking the last drag of the joint when Mia refused it. Mia made her eyes as big as she could.

"Don't pretend to be surprised, Mia," he said. "You're better than that." He flicked the cashed joint into the snirt piled on the sidewalk, where it glowed orange upon impact and then disappeared into its icy depths.

"I don't want to get involved," she told him. "But I wouldn't say that she hates you. 'Hate' is a big word." They locked eyes. "Shit, I guess I just got involved. Me and my big mouth."

What would her husband look like now? Mia wondered, looking at Mitch and noticing his newly receding hairline. Her husband had had a bald spot right in the back of his head, like a bull's-eye. The dudes had the same one, a tiny patch of skin like the tip of a pencil beneath their otherwise luxurious manes.

"I think you should get a dog," Mia told him.

"You think a dog is going to fix us?"

"Maybe?"

"You're tripping," he told her. "And anyway, I'm allergic."

"Shit," said Mia.

"I'm freezing my underutilized balls off out here," Mitch announced, ending the conversation and running for the door.

MIA LAY ON the sofa bed that Rachel had made for her and stared
at the ceiling. She was high. It was a familiar feeling, the feeling of
being light as air, both in body and in mind, but she couldn't accept it. She couldn't accept this kind of manufactured happiness.
It felt disloyal to her grief. She had fought it all night, but still it
fought back, like a game of Whack-A-Mole.

Dinner had been pizza on TV trays in front of a movie that Mia
had never seen but had swept the award season like a tsunami. Rachel and Mitch moved like robots, clearing and cleaning without
saying a word to each other. They'd had Mitch's homemade apple
pie for dessert. Well, Mitch and Mia had.

People were so lucky to be married, Mia thought as the movie
droned on. They were so lucky to be alive. Why were they so sad?
Why didn't they do anything about it?

Mia had a headache now, a headache and a stomachache. She
hadn't eaten that much food in a long time. She pressed against her
stomach under the comforter and sighed. She was always sighing.

Shut up, she told herself. She uncurled her toes; she unclenched
her hands. She was tired, tired-in-her-bones tired. She would
sleep. *One, two . . .*

Three.

Mia couldn't see her husband, but she knew he was there—she

felt his presence in the dream. She was in an apartment, was sitting on a stool that wasn't hers.

"Is he still seeing her?" she asked a faceless woman.

The faceless woman didn't answer.

Mia felt his hand at the small of her back, his long tapered fingers. The warmth of them.

She woke up.

"MORNING," MIA SAID to Rachel.

Mia had woken up drenched in sweat. Her unwanted high lingered, along with her heartbreak.

They were standing in her kitchen.

"Morning," said Rachel. She stirred a generous dollop of half-and-half into her coffee. She wore a navy blue pantsuit. On her feet were black combat boots and around her neck three layers of gold.

"Is that a nightgown?" asked Rachel.

Mia looked down, surveying the red plaid landscape of herself.

"It is," she answered.

"I'm not into it," said Rachel.

"To each their own," said Mia, refilling her white mug.

"So I'm heading to class, and then I have office hours, and then I have another class," Rachel told Mia. "I could be back here by six, or I can meet you for a drink at five."

"Duh," said Mia. "Although, are bars even open? With Covid?"

"We can sit outside. Wear your jacket. Are you good on your own today?"

Mia guessed that she was. "Sure."

"How long have you been awake?" asked Rachel.

Mia glanced at the clock on the wall. "Three hours."

"Ew," said Rachel.

"I had the dream again, the one where he's with someone else."

"Not that white lady with the dreads again?" Rachel wrinkled her nose.

"I just don't understand why that's the dream, you know? Like, I get that he's living his best soul life or whatever, but why do I have to see it?"

"You think this is literal?"

"I don't know," said Mia.

"I think it's your subconscious telling you it's time to date again."

"Gross!" exclaimed Mia. "I have no interest."

"Jews don't even believe in heaven—how are you telling me that he's with someone else in the afterlife?"

"No, I don't think that's it," said Mia. "Sometimes I worry that he settled for me. I wasn't his type. Not really, anyway. I was a prude. I didn't go to yoga with him. I'm not spontaneous. I make outlines for my outlines. His life was so short. I wish he could have been with someone who really made him happy." Mia had never said those words out loud, but she had thought them before.

"Sit your ass down," said Rachel, pointing to the couch.

"What? I—"

"Now."

Mia sat.

"He chose you. He adored you, even a blind person could have seen that. Maybe his younger self wanted a nymphomaniac yogi, but who he was when he met you wanted you. He would have been a fool not to, and he knew that."

Mia took a sip of her coffee. Rachel made sense; she almost always did.

"Think about how many times you saw each other on the train. Years went by, right?"

Mia nodded.

"You were dating every loser that walked through the door during those years."

"Well, not *every* loser," said Mia. "I was selective."

"Barely. Anyway, he was too. Aren't you glad you didn't marry who you thought you wanted before you met him?"

"Yes," answered Mia.

"Well, he was too. Timing, girl. Timing was on your side. You needed to date all those losers to figure out what you didn't want. He did too."

"But I feel guilty," said Mia. "He could have had more fun. I'm not that fun."

"I think he had just what he wanted. And I know that you know that because you had just what you wanted too."

"But would we have made it? People's wants change. Look at you and Mitch."

"I don't know," said Rachel. "I think you would have worked hard at it, because you work hard at everything."

"But you're not working hard at it," said Mia. "And you're an even bigger masochist than I am."

Rachel looked at her watch.

"I gotta go," she told her. She grabbed her black down coat and zipped herself into it, wound her chartreuse scarf around her neck, pulled her gray beanie over her ears. "You're right, Mia, I'm not. I work hard enough. At my job, which I have. You feel me?"

"Can we talk about it later?" Mia asked her.

"Yes." Rachel grabbed her bag and slung it over her shoulder.

"You promise?"

"Yes."

Mia wanted to fix Rachel's marriage so badly. She wanted to help Rachel the way Rachel always helped her.

But who did Mia think she was, anyway, some sort of widow prophet, spouting knowledge from the other side?

The truth was that she did think that. On her good days, anyway. She knew things that her friends didn't. She knew that they all had a clock ticking on their lives, an expiration date that was out of their control. Once you knew that, your entire perception of the world changed. It was a conscious choice every single day to find joy, and so if Rachel and Mitch's joy was just out of their reach, because of circumstance and not incompatibility, Mia had to try to save it.

She had to try, and so she would.

CHAPTER 12

 "Want to grab a coffee?" Mitch asked.

The city was bustling at ten A.M., that specific urban energy of places to go and people to see, all on foot. All wrapped in fleece and down like haute couture penguins. Mia's already caffeinated intestines sloshed as she walked beside him through the bitter cold.

"Sure," she answered.

They ducked into a small shop, blasted by its manufactured warmth and the smell of cinnamon upon entry. Mia felt young again, just for a second. She had frequented many a coffee shop in her former life. But which former life? The one before the dudes or the one before her husband's death? Or the one between her mother's death and her husband's death? She had emerged as a different human each time. Almost, anyway. Her core was still the same.

Mia looked up to find Mitch staring at her expectantly.

"What?" she asked. "Sorry, I spaced."

"Do you want to get hot dogs for lunch?"

"Uh, sure. That's right, Chicago dogs are different. Ketchup is illegal or something?"

"That's right."

In front of them in the line a woman leaned against her partner, her back against his chest.

"What do you think their story is?" she asked Mitch quietly.

"Definitely not married," he said. "Married people don't cuddle. Maybe not even dating? Maybe a one-night thing?"

"But she's leaning on him," Mia pointed out.

"Yes, but look at his stance," Mitch countered. The man's boots were spread wide apart to support her weight; his butt in his skinny jeans was visibly clenched. "He doesn't want to be here, I can tell you that much."

"Maybe he just has to poop," said Mia.

"Nah, I recognize a trapped man when I see one."

"But why bother getting coffee with her at all, then?"

"Why not? It's probably on his way to work."

"Men," said Mia.

Don't say you're going to call when you know that you're not going to call, she had told the dudes.

Okay, they had answered dutifully, not knowing at all what their mother was talking about but sensing her seriousness.

She and Mitch stepped forward in the line.

Before her husband, Mia had dated the free world, but the word *boyfriend* had never come out of her mouth. None of those other men had acted like a boyfriend, but she wasn't sure now, in retrospect, if that had been their fault or hers.

"Were you ever in love before Rachel?" she asked Mitch.

"Nah, not really," he answered. "There were girlfriends, but Rachel was the first real deal. And the last. Maybe."

"How was she different?" asked Mia, ignoring his *maybe*.

"She was so strong. She is so strong, rather. To be needed by her felt like an honor. Plus, she's just so damn fun. Hanging out with her was so much better than being by myself."

Mia nodded. She knew what he meant. She had gotten very good at being alone by the time she had finally introduced herself to her husband, so it had been a shock when being with him was the better option.

"She told me that she loved me first," Mitch told Mia. "I had been in love with her since the moment I met her, but for her to say it first, that was really something."

"She did?" asked Mia. Rachel hadn't told her that. "Where were you, when she told you?"

"In bed. Where else?" Mitch grinned at her. "Those were the days, man."

"Weren't they something?" agreed Mia.

She had imagined what it would feel like to be on the receiving end of those words, but they were no match for the real thing. Her husband had been the first to say them to her. To know that he was invested in her as much as she was invested in him!

It was Mitch and Mia's turn in line; the ill-fated couple had ordered oat-milk lattes.

"Latte with cow milk, whole fat," Mia told the barista with a ring through his septum. "Please."

"And I'll just have a coffee," said Mitch. "Black."

"You're a classicist," said Mia as they shuffled to the next line.

"I like my coffee like I like my women. What can I say?"

"Terrible joke," said Mia.

"I know. Awful. Forgive me. I told you that I can't write any-more." He shook his head.

"Of course you can still write," said Mia. "Writer's block is bullshit."

"No it's not!" argued Mitch. "What's going on with me is very real, believe me. It's like I've forgotten how to be funny."

"No," said Mia. "Writing is like anything else. If you don't show up every day, no matter what, your muscles are going to go slack. I can't tell you how many mornings I sit down at my desk and type garbage. It can be terribly discouraging, but if I sit down every day, if I push through the garbage, I get to the good stuff."

"Mitch? Maya?" the barista proclaimed, setting their steaming cups on the counter.

"It's Mia," she told him, even though she knew he didn't care.

"You write every day?" Mitch asked as they plunged back into the cold.

"Every day. It's my therapy. I don't do yoga or meditation—shit, I don't even stretch, although I should. It's always been my release. And it's always been free, so?" She took a sip, relishing the luxury of a to-go cup. She could never drink coffee and walk at the same time with the dudes in tow.

"Why, how often do you write?" she asked him.

"Not every day. Not even every other day." He began to walk north, and Mia followed. Another luxury: not being in charge.

"So what do you do, then?" she asked him.

"I'm trying to write a screenplay. There's a lot of thinking involved, you know?" He was faster than Mia; his legs were long because he was tall. Her husband had been tall.

"Rachel's not the woman I married," he confessed suddenly.

"Well, thank God for that," said Mia. "It's been how many years? Seven?"

"Ten."

Time passed so quickly when it was happening to other people.

"Ten years is a long time," said Mia. "Haven't you changed?"

"Not really. I'm the same guy, just fatter, really. And technically unemployed. She's an entirely different human. And it's not even like we have kids to blame."

"What's different about her?" asked Mia.

"Well, she hates me, for one."

"She doesn't hate you," said Mia again.

Mitch raised a generous eyebrow at her. "She doesn't want to do anything; she doesn't want to go anywhere. Not with me, anyway. I always feel like I'm annoying her."

"That's a terrible way to feel," said Mia. "I'm sorry."

"I'm thinking about leaving her," he confessed.

Mia's mouth dropped open like a mailbox. "No!"

"Mia, I'm tired of feeling like a schmuck every day. She makes me feel horrible about myself, like I'm not even worthy of taking up space on the planet, much less in our apartment. It's awful."

"No, you can't. The love is there, Mitch. She just wants you to get a job. Why can't you get a job? What do you do all day?"

"I told you: I write sometimes. I think. I bake. I cook. I do all the bullshit. That's a job!"

"Trust me, I know," said Mia. "But you still need to contribute financially or else she can't respect you. It's not like paying the bills and doing the laundry takes up the whole day, Mitch. Come on."

"Why should I be with someone who makes me feel like my job is a hobby? I'm a working writer, just not at this moment. There's no stability in the creative field. That's why you marry a professor. Or a lawyer. Or a hedge fund manager." Mitch sighed.

"I'm not going to leave her," he told Mia. "I just wanted to say it out loud and see what it felt like. But I am really fucking tired of being told that I'm a loser."

"Why can't you get a part-time job?" asked Mia. "I had no idea that you had such a massive ego."

"I pee sitting down. I have no ego." He stopped walking and finished his coffee.

Mitch was handsome, Mia realized. Not in a she-wanted-to-have-sex-with-him way, but more in an *oh, he is actually capable of having sex* kind of way. If he and Rachel split up, he would meet someone new. Mia felt this truth deeply.

Did Rachel know this like Mia knew this? Mia didn't think that she did.

"Then take a job at Costco or something just to bring in some money while you write your screenplay at night," Mia advised him.

"You want me to work at Costco?"

"Yeah, if that's what it takes. Listen, I know how hard it is to make a living as a writer, believe me. It's a joke. That's why you have to pad it with some stability. And it doesn't have to be Costco, obviously. Any place, really."

She was giving Mitch the same talk her parents had given her, the same advice that had launched her teaching career. She ran a writers' group four times a year. It wasn't much money, but it was money she could count on. As an author she only got paid when she signed a contract and when she delivered the finished product. That was an enormous gap without pay.

"Hey, have you ever thought about teaching screenwriting?" she asked Mitch.

"Wanna go into a shop?" he asked.

It was irritating, how Mitch kept dodging her questions, as though she'd never asked them at all. She felt for Rachel.

"What? Sure."

Mia followed him through a green door and into a psychedelic cornucopia of taxidermy, muskets, turquoise, and maps.

"Where are we?" she asked him. "Are there mushrooms in my coffee?" She peered into her half-empty cup. A giraffe wearing a red wool scarf towered over her.

"I love this store," said Mitch. "It's weird without being twee."

Mia walked carefully, not wanting to break anything, to a glass display of human vertebrae bones and peered inside.

"It's something, all right," she said.

"Are you writing anything?" Mitch asked her, tentatively touching a sizable chunk of melon-colored coral reef.

"I'm trying to get a new book idea off the ground," she answered. "But it's hard to work on a new book when you're out promoting the old one."

"A problem I would love to have," said Mitch. "I read your book, by the way. I really liked it."

"You did? Thanks, Mitch."

"Readers know who you are, Mia. That's a big deal in the book world."

"Not enough people," said Mia, wandering into the next room. She hadn't browsed with a straight male, alone, since her husband had died. God, she missed taking it for granted.

Mitch held a magnifying glass to his eye. It was bluish-gray, like the ocean.

"I was out of work for a while. I know how bad it can feel," Mia told him.

Mia had written her third book while she'd been pregnant with their first dude, in between googling crib dimensions and nursing bras. It wasn't that she hadn't tried—she had—but she'd been too distracted. And happy.

The book had bombed. Big time. Mia's agent had had to beg, borrow, and steal to get Mia another deal, but the message was clear: knock the next one out of the park or else. And Mia had. She'd earned back her advance within its first six months on the shelves.

"Hey, look, masks," said Mitch. They hung in various patterns from a doll-size coatrack. "We should get a couple. I don't think this pandemic is going anywhere."

"You buy it? It's really happening?"

"It's happening all right. You reading the news?"

"Not really." She selected a chambray mask and held it up to the light. "I need one, huh?"

"We all do. Here, it's on me." He took it from her. "Which one of these would Rachel like, do you think?"

"That one," she said, pointing to one in leopard print.

"Okay," he said, looping its strings over his ring finger and proceeding to the register, where a woman in pigtails and a red-and-white gingham mask of her own rang him up. Mia didn't understand grown women who wore their hair in pigtails. How did they not look ridiculous to themselves?

Her phone rang.

"Mom, do you have Kimono?" her younger asked, staring at her accusingly.

"It's not Kimono, it's Corona!" her elder yelled.

"I don't think so," answered Mia. "I feel good. I'm being careful, see?" She put on her mask.

"School is closed!" he told her. "We're doing Grandpa School instead."

"Oh boy," said Mia. "Grandpa School is very serious, I bet."

"So serious!" her younger complained. "I'm multiplying."

"Get out," said Mia.

"Mia," said her father, taking the phone.

There was a tone to his voice. She hadn't heard it since he had called to tell her that her mother was sick.

Pancreatic cancer is a death sentence, he had warned her.

"Grandpa, where are you going?" yelled her elder, panic in his voice.

"The backyard! Jesus Christ. I'll be right back!" Ira gazed at her. Brow hairs curled around the tops of his black-framed glasses like grape vines. "I can't go anywhere alone!" he complained.

"Welcome to my life," said Mia.

"It's enough already."

"Dad, their father went to work one morning and never came home. I think the situation requires delicacy."

"You know what?" Ira asked.

"What?"

"You're right."

"Excuse me?"

"You're right. This is a delicate situation, and I don't envy you. But I also know that there's no one more qualified on this planet to do what you have been forced to do. You are a fighter; you've always been a fighter, and I know that you'll fight to the death for these dudes. I've never seen anything like it. It's a love affair between you and them. It always has been."

"Thanks, Dad," said Mia through the lump in her throat. Never did praise affect her more than when it came from her father. Because she knew that he meant it. Her mother too, but now she was gone, and Ira was all she had left.

"You know, I think this Covid thing is all bullshit, but Judy doesn't. She doesn't want me flying home," Ira volunteered suddenly.

"What?" barked Mia.

Shit.

Judy was right. The voice of reason. Pretending that Covid didn't exist was a luxury that Mia could no longer afford. She had just read that morning that older people were more susceptible to infection, that the likelihood of their dying from Covid was much greater. Her father couldn't go out like that, because of her selfishness. Everything as Mia knew it was changing. Again.

"Judy's right. Of course you can't fly. You're old."

"I'm old," he agreed. "So what do we do?"

"You stay with me indefinitely," said Mia. "We'd love to have you."

Mia did not know if she would love to have him, but of course she would have him anyway.

"Judy wants me home," he said. "And I want to go home."

"Okay," said Mia. "Fair enough. So are you going to rent a car and drive back to Atlanta?"

She thought of her father on the road, how he crept along at a snail's pace and crossed wide swathes of highway without even glancing in his rearview mirror. She couldn't let him drive.

"Wait, never mind."

"So you'll drive up with Judy, it's settled, then. Great," he said, his voice lighter.

"Wait, what?" asked Mia. "Who said anything about driving up with Judy?"

"Come on now, Mia, she can't make that drive alone. She barely knows how to pump gas."

"And whose fault is that?" asked Mia.

"You fly to Atlanta tomorrow as expected and then you cancel your flight to Newark. Judy's going to have the Corolla serviced. The bad news is that it will take you thirteen hours to get to us, but the good news is that you'll at least have company and no one will die."

"I can't assure you of that," said Mia.

"Don't be fresh," said Ira.

CHAPTER 13

MIA SAT AT THE CROWDED BAR IN HER HAT, scarf, jacket, and two pairs of gloves, the wine in her glass shaking in her quivering hands. Its owner had opened all three of the giant windows at the front, as well as the entry and exit doors, in an attempt to ward off infection and welcome end-of-the-world bar tabs.

Mia had only come close to experiencing this specific kind of desperation once. It had been a blisteringly hot summer day in New York, so hot that her flip-flops had melted into the asphalt on her way into work. She had been making herself a terrible coffee in the break room when it happened; she had whacked the machine two times before realizing that it wasn't its fault. A colleague ran by in the dim light but then jogged back.

"Blackout!" she had yelled at Mia. "Take the stairs!"

And so Mia had dropped her cup in the trash and run for her bag like the building was on fire. In the post-9/11 era, no one was messing around. Down the staircase she went, crowded into the armpits of everyone who worked in her skyscraper, big-timers and underlings alike, all fighting spastically for the same threshold.

She'd spent the next three hours walking back to Brooklyn through the crowds of people eating free bodega ice cream out of cartons with plastic spoons; the kids dancing in the spray of unleashed fire hydrants, the smokers double fisting.

Is this the end of the world? she had wondered, drenched in sweat underneath her backpack as she marched through the East Village. She was twenty-six; home was a brownstone she had shared with two roommates.

It hadn't been. The sun had risen the next day, just like it always did.

"This is nuts," a voice whispered in her ear.

Rachel pulled a stool over and sat, holding her enormous burgundy leather satchel on her lap like a child.

"Did you order this for me?" She pointed to the bourbon neat in front of her. "That was sweet. Thanks."

"I wonder what it's like to be single right now," said Rachel as they observed the crowd.

"I'm single," said Mia.

"Not really. You have the dudes."

Mia drained her wine. "Boy, do I," she said. "I spoke to my dad, by the way. He wants me to drive up with Judy instead of flying."

"Whoa," said Rachel. "I mean, that's the safe thing to do. But can you be nice for that long?"

"I guess we'll see," said Mia.

"The vibe here reminds me of the blizzards we used to get in Boston," said Rachel. "Remember those?"

"Remember when they closed down Comm Ave?" Mia asked.

What shoes had she worn then? Mia wondered now. She couldn't remember having any snow boots. She also could not for the life of her remember where she had done her laundry, although of course she had done it. Right?

"God, youth really does make you invincible," she told Rachel.

"I know that's right," she agreed. "So, you ready for tonight?"

"Born ready," said Mia. "It's a dinner and a signing?"

"Yeah, with my department." Rachel was an English professor. "It will be chill, but also not at all. We all read your memoir. We bought your memoir, I should say."

"There is a difference. Thanks, man," said Mia.

"Mitch is just going to meet us there, I think."

"Yeah, that's what he said earlier. He took me to the weirdest little shop."

"Woolly Mammoth," said Rachel. "He loves that place." She finished her bourbon and slammed it on the bar.

"You okay?"

"I don't know," said Rachel. "Everything he does annoys me, Mia. It's not good."

"But why? He's so nice."

"Sure he's nice, but nice is not enough, I don't think. Or is it?" She stood up. "Is it easier to just be complacent?"

Mia thought about how much harder her life was without her husband.

"Maybe? I don't know," she told her. "I just can't believe that you don't love him anymore. Not even a teensy bit? Maybe if he had a job you would love him?"

"See, that's what I don't know. Maybe? But probably not?"

"So let him get a job and then see what's what," said Mia as they left the bar.

There had been a three-month window when her husband hadn't worked; he'd just defended his thesis and had declared that he *needed a break*. Mia had been working full time and writing on the weekends at the time. She'd had no patience for his break. *You have to get a job!* she had yelled at him. *Who takes breaks?*

The things she would have changed if only she had known.

"C'mon," said Rachel. "It's this way."

"But even if he did get a job, it's his entitlement that kills me," said Rachel as fluffy flakes of snow melted into their jackets. "I would never be okay not holding up my half of the bargain. I was working at fifteen! How can he even like himself right now?"

"He probably doesn't," said Mia. "Well, maybe he does. Men seem to be so much easier on themselves than women are."

"That's what I'm saying! The breaks he cuts himself, damn! White male energy all the way. He wasn't like this when I met him."

It was the same complaint Mitch had had about Rachel, both of them outraged that they'd been bamboozled out of the truth by their hormones. But the fact of the matter was that no one wanted to know the truth, not really.

Mia knew this because kindergarten had begun for her older dude five months after her husband had died. At pickup, an unassuming mom with beach waves had asked Mia how she was. *I'm terrible, I can't sleep at night, my husband is dead,* she had told her. Beach Waves Mom had a blunt bob now, but she still wouldn't make eye contact with Mia, three years later.

"We're here," said Rachel, stopping in front of a modernized brownstone, one that looked warm inside. Mia envisioned a glass of red wine in her hand, sitting on the couch that backed up to the window.

"I thought we would be in the school cafeteria or something," said Mia. "This is so nice. Is it someone's apartment?"

"I wouldn't do you dirty like that, come on now. This is Gwen Galloway's place. She's hosting."

"Gwen Galloway like, *the* Gwen Galloway?"

"That's the one."

"Wait, you didn't tell me that she was teaching with you!" said Mia, following her up the stairs. Gwen had been the talk of the town two years prior; her debut novel had sold for six figures, Mia had read.

"Yep."

"Is she cool?" Mia asked.

"Not really," Rachel said, and rang the doorbell. "But I heard she can cook."

JEALOUSY WAS A useless emotion. It had no purpose other than to make Mia feel bad and act worse. It never fueled her creativity, not the way love and hate and sadness did. She wrote to lose it, not to follow it. And still, walking up the stairs of Gwen Galloway's brownstone—she owned an entire brownstone!—jealousy wrapped its sinuous legs around Mia's waist and its wiry arms around her neck, making it hard to breathe.

"You all right?" Rachel asked. "You look kind of green."

"Yeah, I'm fine," Mia told her.

Rachel rang the doorbell and let herself in. On a wooden bench by the door sat a yellow ceramic bowl filled with blue masks. She took one for herself and handed another to Mia.

So this was how it was going to be now. At least she didn't have to worry about lipstick.

Promise me you'll wear lipstick, her mother had demanded. From her deathbed, no less.

"Hello!" A man in a brown corduroy suit greeted Rachel with a wave.

"Hi, Stanley. Stanley, Mia. Mia, Stanley. Stanley is the dean," she explained to Mia. "And Mia is, of course, the author."

"A pleasure," said Stanley. He led them into the party, the kind of party that Mia had not attended in many years. A work party. Groups of two and three huddled around each other awkwardly, their masks sucking into their mouths as they spoke.

"Mia!"

She turned to find Gwen Galloway beaming at her, her brown eyes bright. She was so young. Jealousy wound around her torso now, like a python. She wasn't even forty years old, and look what she had done. A brownstone. Teaching at Northwestern.

Go away, Mia told the python, but it squeezed tighter. Mia could feel its cold, wet, and scaly skin against the back of her neck.

"Gwen," she said. "It's so nice to meet you. Thank you for hosting this in a pandemic of all the things!" Mia's voice was shrill and deep, the way it always was when she was nervous.

"I love your writing," Gwen told her.

"You do?" The snake slithered into the muted tones of the Persian rug beneath their feet, lost in its threads.

"Of course. I've been reading you since the beginning. Your first book, about the lifeguard?"

"That was my second," said Mia. "But it doesn't matter. Thank you. Thank you very much."

"Come, let's get you a drink," Gwen said. They made their way to her kitchen, past the wall of bookshelves filled with intention, around the dining room table that had once been a door, the kind of table that Mia coveted but would never have the money to buy.

"Red, please," she told Gwen, who filled her glass to the top.

"This is my husband, Paul," said Gwen, squeezing his shoulder. "He's still alive."

"What's that?" said Mia.

"Oh, I just said that he's a writer too."

"Nice to meet you," said Mia.

"I loved your book," she told Gwen. "How did you manage that plot? You had me the whole way through."

This was not entirely true, but mostly true. Mia knew how hard it was to keep a plot going; she knew because she had certainly failed at it before.

"Thank you," said Gwen. "It took me six years to see it through, six years and a hell of an editor."

"God bless editors," said Mia.

Mitch joined them at the bar for a moment, pouring himself a bourbon with a nod and then wandering away, a plate filled with cheese cubes and crackers in his other hand. Mia searched the room for Rachel. She stood by the crackling fireplace, flanked on both sides.

"What are you working on now?" she asked Gwen.

"Ugh, it's a disaster," said Gwen. "I can't get past the first chapter."

"Do you have an outline?"

"Oh no, I don't do outlines," said Gwen. "I'm a visual writer. A giant bulletin board, note cards, that kind of thing."

"Like you're solving a murder?"

"Exactly."

"Can I see?"

"Sure. My office is upstairs. Come on."

They took the stairs, stopping for a moment to admire Gwen's reading nook on the landing. Soft jewel-toned pillows rested on a daybed built under the window. Mia had always wanted a reading nook. The snake returned, slithering around her wrist.

"So here it is," said Gwen, opening the door.

It was exactly as Mia had imagined it would be. An imposing wooden desk facing a wall of thumbtacked words. A laptop and a desktop on which an array of Gwen's world travels floated across the screen: one exotic adventure after the other.

More books lined the walls. A couch for naps.

Mia wrote at an IKEA table dinged with the remnants of meals once served. Marker graffiti from the dudes crawled up its legs.

"It's beautiful," said Mia.

"Thanks," said Gwen. "It's the office I dreamed of as a kid."

"Lucky," said Mia. "So what's your new book about?"

"Oh God, I don't even know," answered Gwen. "It's supposed to be about Socrates, but it's just a mess. I can't figure out my protagonist's motivation for the life of me, which probably means that I need a new idea."

"Probably," agreed Mia. "Have you tried writing her—I assume it's a her?—in scenes outside of your plot? That helps me sometimes, to imagine her as a three-dimensional person outside of my outline. You know, at the grocery store or something."

"It's a he," said Gwen. "My protagonist. I wanted to challenge myself, but it's not working out. I can't imagine being a man, and so everything he says falls flat."

"Have you fleshed out his backstory? Given him reasons to be how he is?"

"No," said Gwen. "That's a good idea." She nodded. "Maybe his mother was fucked up or something, you mean?"

"Aren't we all?" asked Mia.

"So is that what you do when your writing sucks?" asked Gwen. "You take a time-out from the plot and create the why?"

"Yeah," said Mia.

"Do you love writing?" asked Gwen. "Like really love it, can't live without it?"

"I do," said Mia. "Nothing makes me feel better."

"Even when you suck?"

"Well, maybe not when I suck. But sticking with it through the suck—that's the stuff."

"I'm not sure that I love it," confessed Gwen.

"But your writing, it's so good."

"I worry that I'm a one-hit wonder," said Gwen. "A fraud. A lucky fraud, but a fraud just the same. Mia was both startled and charmed by Gwen's honesty. "I don't think I have it in me to go the distance, not like you have. I'm nervous," said Gwen. "I sit down to write, and it's all just blah. Blah blah blah. It's not like it was the first time."

"Nothing is ever going to be like the first time," said Mia. "You have to give yourself space. And time. You have to lean into the suck to climb out of it."

The suck. Mia had been there so many times, convinced that she couldn't write it back to life. And then she had.

"Everyone says don't write what you know," said Gwen. "But you did."

"Well, it's a memoir, to be fair. And I didn't have a choice," said Mia. "Grief will eat you alive if you don't get it out. And who's everyone? Your college writing professor?"

"Hey, I'm a college writing professor," joked Gwen. "And yes. And the critics. So many critics."

"Fuck them," said Mia. "I can't write any other way. You can't fake heart. I can't, anyway."

Mia thought of the dudes. Her whole heart, out there in the world walking around.

Day by day.

Character by character. Plot by plot. It was all the same.

"You're lucky," Gwen told her.

"Oh yeah?" Mia snorted. "How so?"

"Well, in terms of material for your writing, anyway."

"What do you mean?" asked Mia, a chill creeping up her spine.

"Things have happened to you. You should write what you know because a lot of us don't know what you know."

"I'm lucky that my husband died?"

"Well, not lucky," said Gwen, laughing nervously. "That's the wrong word."

"You're goddamn right that's the wrong word."

Gwen held up her hands in surrender. "Oh God, that's not what I meant to say. I'm sorry. I meant to say that you're so wise; that you have so much to teach the rest of us, having gone through what you went through. That's all."

"I would surrender my writing career in an instant if it meant my husband had gotten to live," she told Gwen. "I'd rather not know and be writing about the mundane. Believe me."

"I believe you," said Gwen. "Forgive me. This pandemic has me all turned inside out. I can't write and apparently, I also can't speak."

"It's okay," Mia told her.

People said the dumbest shit to her sometimes. Like a mom friend, who had said *But you get to start over now!* with wistful wonder one afternoon when Mia was mourning, when she had barely been able to get out of bed. People meant well, but grief was tricky from the outside.

It was true, Mia would have given up her writing for her husband's life. The two greatest loves of her life but it was no contest. The dudes needed him so badly.

She had gotten her first book deal right after she had gotten engaged. In shock and disbelief, she had had to put her head between her legs to breathe. *How could she be this lucky?* she had asked herself at the time. She wasn't lucky. How could she have a writing career and be madly in love? It was too much happiness.

She had pushed that voice out of her head and gotten married; and published books; and had two beautiful children; all the while marveling at her bounty. It had felt like luck, but she had been raised as unlucky and so she would question her staying power sometimes, staring at the ceiling when she couldn't sleep.

Mia had been right of course, but she wished with all of herself that she hadn't been.

"My advice?" she said to Gwen now.

"Yes, please."

"Do your best and fuck the rest. It's the only way to be a real anything, much less a writer."

"Like you," said Gwen.

"Yeah. Like me."

"WHERE YA BEEN?" asked Mitch. Mia picked a cube of Cheddar from his plate and ate it.

"Checking out Gwen's office."

"You sneak in?"

"No, with her."

"How is she?"

"She was cool," said Mia. "I wanted to despise her, but I don't."

"I hate it when that happens," said Mitch.

"Everyone?" Gwen announced, holding a butter knife like a microphone. "Shall we move to the dining room?"

The group of eleven—Mia had counted them—complied, moving to Gwen's table like a school of salmon. Assigned seating and Mia was at the head. She needed a water. Stat.

"Welcome, everyone, to what may be our last gathering before the world implodes," Gwen told the table. "I've seated you as far away from each other as possible while still keeping you at the actual table; the windows are open." She shrugged. "Let's hope for the best, shall we?"

"That's all we can do," said a woman in red.

Mia had taken off her jacket but had left her husband's mint-green scarf wound around her neck. He had loved scarves and wore them like some kind of Prussian king, looped around his long neck and tied haphazardly, not quite European but close enough. It still smelled like him.

It didn't feel real, it didn't feel possible that people had come here to see Mia, that they were actually interested in her perspective, that she had a perspective at all. She would always second-guess whether she had anything important to say, but her compulsion to write overrode her uncertainty. Every time.

She was grateful. Feeling grateful was different now that she was a widow; it had a weight to it. A weight she was strong enough to carry.

"What's up with Gwen Galloway's eye contact?" Rachel asked Mia. They were on her couch, sharing a bag of Twizzlers and a bottle of white wine. "Do you think she's overcompensating? Like maybe she had a lazy eye as a kid?"

"Maybe," said Mia. "Or maybe it's just her thing, you know? Like a firm handshake."

"It makes me uncomfortable," said Rachel.

"Well, you don't forget her, that's for sure. She was actually cool," said Mia.

"Oh yeah? We don't interact much," said Rachel.

"Why not?"

"Too bougie. Did you see her house? It was like living in a Restoration Hardware catalog."

"I liked it," said Mia.

"She always does this thing, when I'm around," said Rachel. "She talks like I talk."

"What do you mean?"

"She talks like a black woman," said Rachel. "It's embarrassing."

"What? How?" Mia recognized herself in Rachel's critique.

"She's like, *Hey, girl!* whenever I approach. The cadence of her voice changes. I'm like, *You are white.* It's okay to be white in front of a black person. You know?"

"Shit," said Mia. "I do that."

"You do," agreed Rachel.

"I'm sorry," said Mia. "It's only because I think you're so much cooler than I am. You sound cooler, you look cooler, you dance cooler. Do I have to stop?"

"You probably should. I don't mind because I love you, but a different black person might not feel that way."

"What are you guys talking about?" asked Mitch, walking in from the bedroom.

"White people talking like black people," Rachel explained.

"Oh," said Mitch knowingly. "Yeah. I see it all the time. Or hear it, rather."

"You never did it? Accidentally or something?" Mia asked him.

"No," said Mitch. "I'm way too cool for that."

"Yeah, right," said Rachel. "The first time you had me over, D'Angelo was on the stereo."

"Stereo!" said Mia. "God, we're old."

"I happen to like D'Angelo," said Mitch. "It was my go-to make-out music, regardless of color."

"Whatever you say," said Rachel, smiling.

"What? It was!" Mitch opened the refrigerator and stared into it.

"I'll do better," Mia told Rachel. "I'm mortified. I thought black people liked me. Wait, is that racist what I just said? It's racist, isn't it? Shit."

"Kind of. But I like you, and I'm black."

"What about me?" asked Mitch, pulling out a carton of milk.

"Yeah, you're all right," said Rachel.

"I'm *aight*," said Mitch.

"Stop it right now." Rachel was laughing.

Mitch pulled a box of Cheerios out of the pantry, pulled a bowl down from the shelf. Mia's husband had been a night cereal person too. She could see him pacing and crunching as he ate, dimly lit by the light of the television. God, she missed him.

"Guys," said Mia.

"What?"

"You can't go down without a fight."

Mitch put his bowl down on the counter.

"You have to try harder to save this. You guys love each other, I know that you do."

"What are you, our daughter?" asked Mitch.

"I know, it's weird, but I can't not say anything while I'm here. I know that you're having problems. I also know that you can fix them."

"By getting a job," said Rachel.

"It's not just the job," said Mia.

"Thank you, Mia," said Mitch. He threw his bowl in the sink and then thought better of it and shoved it into the dishwasher.

"Those are clean!" said Rachel.

"See, that's what I'm talking about. I can never do anything right with her. She always has something to say! It's fucking emasculating as hell, and I'm tired of it." He collapsed into the orange chair and put his head in his hands. "I'm tired."

"*You're tired?*" yelled Rachel. "I work twelve-hour days and come home to you watching basketball, in the same clothes I left you in! You should feel emasculated!"

"What do you know about being an artist?" Mitch asked her accusingly. "You are the least creative person I've ever met in my life. A writer doesn't need to get dressed up, Rachel. And I don't just sit on my ass and watch basketball. Who do you think does the shopping and the cooking around here? A magician?"

"Are you guys in therapy?" Mia asked them.

"No," said Rachel. "I don't believe in therapy."

"Oh yeah, because this is really working," said Mitch. "We're really communicating here." He looked at Mia. "Meanwhile, my sister is a psychologist, so it's a big middle finger to my family when she says that."

"Mitch, why won't you get a job?" Mia asked him.

"I don't want to work some bullshit job just to bring in a paltry salary," he told her. "I like doing the cooking."

"I don't give a shit about food!" Rachel yelled. She stood up. "I need an equal here, not a chef."

"I just don't see what the big deal is, Rachel. We're fine financially."

"We are not fine!" said Rachel. "I want to travel. I want to buy nice things. That's what we said we wanted instead of kids! Do you remember how hard I worked to get my Ph.D.? How many times I wanted to quit? Remember that adjunct job? We could barely afford ramen. And what's up with you, Mia, coming here like Dr. Phil?"

"Dr. Phil?" asked Mia. "That's a low blow."

Mia looked at Mitch looking at Rachel and decided to have somewhere else to be. She got up carefully, taking her glass of wine with her.

"Where are you going?" Rachel demanded.

"Your bed."

"With your wine?"

"Yes."

Mia crawled in. The murmur of their argument comforted her. She was seven; she was forty-three; she was a bride; she was a mother; she was a widow. She was alive.

The night before he died, her husband had gone to pick up a new pair of glasses after work, and so Mia had had to feed and clean up and bathe and put the dudes to bed. Her father and Judy had arrived from Atlanta that afternoon, but they had swiftly anchored themselves in front of the television and hadn't moved since.

Just as Mia had collapsed onto the couch, her husband had called. There was a concert at a wine bar nearby.

"Digable Planets!" she could hear him saying, breathless and excited. Mia had been annoyed by his excitement in the face of her exhaustion. "Leave the kids with your parents and come on, let's go," he had pleaded.

"They just got here. I can't just leave them to babysit the first night they're here. And she's not my parent."

Her husband had come home a half hour later, disappointed, to find her on the couch next to her father, who was flossing. A baseball game blared on the television in front of them.

Mia had looked at her husband, had studied his face as he watched the screen, his olive temple flexing with each bite of the lasagna she had baked. He had felt her looking at him, had turned to her and raised his eyebrow mid-chew.

"He's fucking flossing," she had whispered to him about her father.

Her husband had shrugged his shoulders.

"Hey, guys, who has the best voice?" her father asked, draping his used floss over the armrest.

"What do you mean?" snapped Mia.

"The singer with the best voice!" he had barked, impatient. "When you were little, Mia, who was on *Letterman* every time you couldn't sleep?"

"Steve Winwood."

"Yes! Very good!" her father had said. "What a voice."

"Yeah, but what about Jerry Garcia?" her husband had countered.

"Who?" her father had asked.

"No, the best voice in rock and roll is Michael McDonald," Mia had announced.

"Now you're talking," said Ira, clapping her on the back.

Mia would always wish that she had met him at that concert. That she had sucked up her resentment, put on a bra, and danced with him on his last night alive. Instead, he had spent it watching her father floss. These kinds of moments had haunted her, were the reasons why she sometimes doubted whether she had been the right one for him.

Mia realized now that there was only so much she could do. She had to stop beating herself up for being who she was when she didn't know how fragile life was. She had just been doing the best she could. It would always take her breath away just thinking about it, how her husband could have been eating her lasagna one night, gone, really and truly gone, by the next, but she hadn't known. Now she did. That was what her book was about; that was what the book tour that was really a friend tour was about. Trying to get the people she loved—George, Rachel, and Chelsea—to understand what she wished she had known.

MIA WOKE UP and had no idea where she was.

Am I dead? she wondered, and pinched her stomach under her nightgown. It hurt. She was in Mitch and Rachel's bedroom, she remembered now. Why hadn't they moved her? Where were they?

She stood up, dizzy from the wine, her mouth dry and her skin clammy. She would tell them to take the bed and she would go back to the couch. But first, a glass of water.

She turned on the light in the bathroom and jumped, the brightness hurting her eyes. On the counter, a cup. She ran it under the faucet, pausing to marvel at the tiny beard hairs decorating the sink like confetti. She even missed those.

The apartment was silent and dark, save for the city lights

twinkling outside its windows. The sofa bed had been pulled out; on its mattress lay Mitch and Rachel, both naked, their limbs entwined like branches. Their chests rose with their breath, synced in unison.

She tiptoed back to their bedroom and burrowed under the covers. This was what she had wanted for Rachel and Mitch, and this was what had happened. An intersection so rare that it trumped melancholy. And yet.

How she missed sleeping with her husband. He would annoy her and she would irritate him as they accepted the monotony of their everyday as career people and then parents: the chopping of vegetables, the grocery runs, the scrubbing of toilets, the budgets, the bills, the diapers.

And yet the exquisite vulnerability of sex had always brought them back to each other. The specific weight of him. And then afterward, curled into each other, bare and warm. His skin had been so smooth. Like silk.

Mia removed her nightgown and burrowed deeper into the sheets, hugging herself to sleep, pretending it was him.

CHAPTER 14

 MIA TOOK A PHOTO OF HER SUITCASE BY RA-
chel's door.

Look out, Atlanta! she posted to Instagram, needing her glasses
but not wanting to need them.

"Hey, wait," she said to Mitch, who leaned against the kitchen
island with one hand and held his steaming cup of coffee in the
other.

The sleep was still in his eyes, his cowlicks untamed.

"Should I not post about traveling?"

"I mean, it's a little tone-deaf," he offered.

"Shit," said Mia. "I'm glad I asked. That would have been career
suicide."

"Totally," said Mitch.

"My three followers who don't know me personally would jump
ship." She put her phone down and burned the roof of her mouth
on the coffee Mitch had poured her.

"Do you have a lot of pressure to post? From your agent?" Mitch
asked her, grimacing. "What a nightmare."

"It's not my favorite thing," said Mia. "But sometimes it's the only way I can prove to myself that I'm still here, you know?" She thought of George. Had anything changed?

Rachel headed toward them emphatically on her heels, each step an exclamation point.

"Good morning, everyone!"

"You look nice," said Mia, because she did. A camel-colored cashmere turtleneck with a camel-colored corduroy skirt and camel-colored tights.

"You look like a sexy PEZ dispenser," Mitch told her.

"Oh, that's nice," said Rachel. "Thanks, Mitch." She grinned at him, and Mia blushed, remembering how she had found them.

"Did you call your car?" she asked Mia.

"I will now," she answered.

"I hope everything goes okay," said Rachel.

"Meaning I don't catch Covid and die?"

"I was talking about Judy."

After her mother had died, Mia had secretly felt like she was in the clear, like the worst had happened and she was safe. She hadn't told anyone, but she had thought it. Idiot.

"Yeah. Judy." Mia sighed. She had a thirteen-hour car ride with her to endure. "By the way, how was your night?"

"Why are you looking at me like that?" asked Rachel.

"I saw you."

"Having sex?" whispered Rachel.

"No, after. In flagrante."

"Oh God." Rachel shook her head and grinned. "Are you happy now?"

"I am," said Mia. "Are you?"

"You know what? I am too. But he still needs to get a job."

"He will," said Mia. "I love you, Rachel. He does too. Where'd he go, by the way?"

"Pooping. Every day, like clockwork."

"Lucky," said Mia. "Tell him that I said bye and that I'm rooting for him."

"I will not tell him that," said Rachel.

"Okay, well, just bye, then."

"Be careful!" Rachel shouted down the hallway after her.

"See you on the other side!" Mia yelled back, hoping it was true.

CHAPTER 15

MIA SAT BY THE WINDOW AND WATCHED A MAN in an orange vest load baggage into the belly of a plane that was not hers. Hers had yet to pull into the gate.

A two-year-old toddled over to Mia, her jet-black hair pulled back from her face by a navy blue bow.

"Hello," said Mia.

The toddler stood absolutely still and examined Mia. Mia crossed her eyes and wagged her head back and forth. She galloped away, giggling into the arms of her dad.

Her dad.

Don't cry, Mia, come on, she told herself. She sucked the tears back into her heart.

A boy ran his suitcase right over Mia's toes. Mia frowned at him, but he ignored her, enchanted by the McDonald's bags his mother was carrying. When Mia had traveled with her parents, she was not to eat or drink anything under penalty of death, not after the ketchup incident when she was four. She had insisted on opening the tiny packet by herself and promptly doused herself in the process, a gelatinous slash of red across the placket of her blue-and-white-striped blouse.

Mia's phone vibrated in her pocket.

"Hello?" she asked.

"Hello, Mia?" said Judy.

"Yes, this is me. Hi."

"This is who?"

"Me. I'm Mia."

"Oh, I'm so sorry, I must have the wrong number, please forgive me—"

"Judy! It's Mia!"

"Oh gosh, what a morning," said Judy.

Mia glanced at the gate attendant. Could she get Mia out of this? Fly her to New Jersey instead, where she would drive Ira back home with the dudes in tow? Anything to avoid thirteen hours alone with Judy.

"What time can I expect you today?" she asked Mia.

"Oh, I dunno, maybe three? Or four? What time is my thing again?"

"Oh, well, I have no idea, I can check the calendar, hold on." Judy didn't understand the concept of rhetorical.

"No, I know it's at six, just thinking out loud."

"They're still having it?" asked Judy.

"I haven't heard anything to the contrary, but I guess I probably should check. Maybe it's better just not to know, though. Just show up and hope for the best."

"So what time?" asked Judy.

"Four. Let's say four."

"But where are you eating dinner?" Judy asked, alarmed.

"I'll figure it out," Mia told her. "Don't worry."

"But you're staying overnight here, at the house?"

"Yes," said Mia.

"And I'm not worried, it's just that I bought everything to cook. What will I do with all this ground turkey?"

"Freeze it?"

Mia did not give a shit about what Judy was going to do with her turkey. The older people got, the weirder they got about food.

Judy was silent as she considered this. The gate was becoming crowded with masked passengers, gauging their odds of survival.

We're all going to die! Relax! Mia wanted to yell.

"Okay," Judy said carefully. "Yes, I'll put it in the deep freeze. Have you spoken to your father today, by any chance?"

"Judy, it's eight in the morning."

"Well, yes, but they have him up at six," she said, blame in her voice. As though the dudes were not eight- and five-year-olds whose thoughts were never about anyone other than themselves.

"No, I haven't spoken to him," she answered. "Oh, they're calling my flight. See you later!" Mia hung up her phone and shoved it deep into her bag.

Mia cut the line, boarding with business class when she was absolutely not seated there. As long as she believed she belonged at the front of the line, so would everyone else. Her husband had taught her that.

Was it fair? No. But was it thrilling? Yes.

Her mother would not have approved. Mia shoved her suitcase

into the overhead compartment and collapsed into her window seat.

She had been complicated, her mother. She had not been a touchy-feely, play-with-her-kids kind of mother. She was a boss kind of mother, but for good reason: she worked full time and cooked all the meals and washed all the laundry and it wasn't fun, it was a job. She'd liked to talk to Mia, to read with Mia, but never to play with Mia. She'd been so smart, so striking. So different from the other moms.

Mia's seatmates arrived: a mother and her teenage son. She hovered around his every move, reminding Mia of herself. She had to start letting the dudes fend for themselves, she decided, watching the mother buckle his seat belt. After a certain point, that was what good parenting was, but why did it have to be so hard? Because everything worthwhile was hard.

The dudes. Was Ira letting them cry if they wanted to cry? Was he giving them their cut-up apples in the afternoon, after lunch? With scoops of peanut butter on the side? In the special peanut butter bowls?

She knew that Ira was not. She also knew that they were fine.

The plane lifted off, and Mia closed her eyes. There was something about the air pressure in a plane; it forced all her pain to the surface. She always cried during takeoff, even before she'd had anything to cry about.

Her older son had crawled into bed with her the morning after his father had died. He hadn't known. Not yet.

He had curled into the space where his father had slept but never would sleep again, his back soft and tan.

"Can you go get your brother?" she had asked him, her voice barely a whisper. She was not awake yet, but she had also never slept, not really.

"Why?"

"Just go get him, honey."

Down the stairs he had run, *clomp, clomp, clomp*.

"Get up! Mom wants to talk to you!"

A pause.

"Wait, Mom! He's in his crib!"

"Oh," she had said. "Right."

Clomp, clomp, clomp down the stairs Mia went.

She had stood in the very-early-morning light of his room, her elder sitting on the rug and her younger standing on his mattress, his diaper full.

I'm going to have to turn that crib into a twin bed soon, Mia had realized, standing there as they looked up at her expectantly. *And potty train.*

All by myself.

She had walked over to her younger to scoop him up. He had smelled like lavender. So soft, so warm, so sweet nuzzling into her neck.

She settled him and herself on the rug to make a circle of three with his brother.

"Dad died last night," she told them, tears running into her mouth.

That week, as her husband had lain in the hospital, as Mia went from defeated to hopeful to silenced by the reality of what was to come, she had been telling the dudes that the doctors were doing everything they could. Every night, when she came home to put them to bed, she would tell them that before kissing them good night. She had considered bringing them to the hospital to see their dad, but ultimately she hadn't. Mia had wanted his sons to remember him as the force of life that he was. He deserved that.

"There was nothing left to do?" her elder had asked.

"No, honey." She took his hand with her right and her younger's with her left.

"Mama," said the younger. "Why are you sad?"

"Because he died, honey. We'll never see him again."

"Oh," he said.

"But he lives forever in our hearts," Mia told them. "His soul lives in us."

Both of them had considered this thoughtfully, searching her face for answers that weren't there.

"Like God," her elder had decided finally.

Mia had been struck by his perfect wisdom as they lay on the rug afterward, staring up at the wobbly ceiling fan, their warm hands in hers.

Mia opened her eyes as the snack cart rolled by.

She didn't know if she believed in God like her dudes did, but she asked for help anyway.

Just please get me home? she asked. *Please?*

CHAPTER 16

 "MAN, SPRING IS SPRINGIN' DOWN HERE."

Mia slid her window down a crack, and the smell of wet earth, roots, and buds on the verge of bloom filled Chelsea's minivan with color.

Mia hadn't even bothered to notice the glory of the Atlanta spring until she had returned as an adult, escaping the dreary dregs of New York City in March. The way the kudzu clung; how the trees exploded all at once, all overnight; the vibrant pops of yellow and purple and burgundy and pink like a kaleidoscope.

"Mom, do you have Kimono?" her younger had asked her just a few minutes before, and she smiled now, thinking of him.

"So how are you?" she asked Chelsea.

Chelsea sat beside her in the driver's seat, her hands at ten and two precisely, her workout skort grazing her sun-screened thighs. She kept her brown hair out of her face with a blue visor. Being kind was not a choice for Chelsea; it was just who she was.

Chelsea was very practical, not even a little bit interested in clothes she couldn't pick up while she was buying groceries, as well as the most inherently good person Mia had ever met.

"I'm okay!" she answered. She glanced over to Mia and smiled with her whole face, her eyes too. "I'm just so happy to see you."

"Same," said Mia, grinning back at her. "You look good."

"Do I? Thanks, I've been doing CrossFit with Monica. She's lost forty pounds—can you believe it?"

"Forty pounds!" Mia whistled. "Damn."

"Yeah, she got into French cooking there for a while. Not good for anybody."

"River ate escargot?" asked Mia, referring to their notoriously picky eater.

"Of course not. We just made him mac and cheese."

"What's going on with that charter school you were trying to get him into?"

"Did I not tell you? He got in! Praise the lord hallelujah."

"Amazing," said Mia. "Finally, some good news."

River was twelve and had been in and out of therapy since he'd gotten banned from his preschool for biting. His diagnosis was always changing; doctors were always tweaking and then re-tweaking his meds in the hopes that he could be fixed. Mia didn't know what to think—could a kid just be an asshole? Was that a diagnosis?—but she knew enough to keep her mouth shut.

"The only thing is, the school is next to this raunchy motel that popped up out of nowhere. Daily rates, the whole nine. The parents are trying to get it demolished or at the very least moved, but so far nothing."

"Are you on the board?" asked Mia.

"Not yet, but I guess I have to be." Chelsea sighed.

"That reminds me of that hotel we stayed in."

"Shannon's wedding!" said Chelsea. "She's divorced now. A used condom in the sheets! That wasn't ours!" Mia's bare foot had found it.

"Unbelievable," said Mia. "We got our money back, right?"

"Of course we did."

"But why didn't we change rooms?"

"Because we're gross," said Chelsea as she turned into her neighborhood. Mia found it horrifying, just the idea of living in the same town she had grown up in, but it suited Chelsea. She'd gone away to college but then came right back, overjoyed to teach elementary school at the same elementary school where she and Mia had met, thirty-five years prior.

It smells the same! she had texted Mia, and Mia knew exactly what she was talking about: glue and paint with a hint of beefaroni and a dash of bleach.

"House looks good," said Mia. "And the yard, wow."

Layers of bushes and flowers flowed seamlessly into one another around its perimeter, tickling the white brick of the two-story house. A tidy vegetable garden stood in the shade of a stately oak tree.

"Want to see the back?" asked Chelsea. "We did a thing back there."

"A thing? Sure."

She followed Chelsea up the driveway and around the back of her home. A screened-in cedar porch extended the top two floors over a lush, green yard filled with leaves and fronds and sunflowers and irises. An elaborate homemade rope course was strung between two stately oaks, one of which supported a generous tree house.

"Wow," said Mia. "Did you do this?"

"River did the rope and stuff. I did the gardening."

"River built this obstacle course?"

"He likes to build things."

"My dudes can't even open chip bags," confessed Mia.

"Well, at least they're socially competent," said Chelsea. "That will take them a whole lot farther than woodworking, I bet."

"How is River?"

River couldn't control his anger, but not in a tantrum-at-Target kind of way.

More like a destroy-a-display-at-IKEA-by-dumping-Gatorade-on-a-bedspread kind of way. Mia loved him because he was Chelsea's son, but it was very hard to like him.

"He's okay," she said. "We took him off what he was on and now we have something new to try." She sighed.

Mia reached over and squeezed her shoulder. "I'm sorry," she said to Chelsea.

"My parents would say that God's mad at me because I'm a lesbian," she joked.

"Fuck your parents. What does Monica say?"

"Not much. You know how I am."

"I don't get it," said Mia. "Why won't you let her be a parent?"

"Because Monica doesn't get him."

"What's to get? He's her son too."

Chelsea was a do-it-herself kind of person. She liked things done her way because she'd grown up having to do everything everybody else's way.

She hadn't come out of the closet until she was nineteen because she hadn't known that she was in the closet in the first place. Growing up the child of devout Southern Baptists could do that to a person.

"He's a complicated kid. Just Monica's tone of voice sets him off. She doesn't have the patience he requires."

"No one has the patience he requires," said Mia. "Except you. What happens when he goes out in the world?"

"That's exactly the point. The whole world is chaos for him. Why not make his home safe? Calm? When Monica gets involved, all hell breaks loose."

"I love you, but damn," said Mia. "You know how much I would kill for another parent? It's too hard on your own."

"Our family is different, Mia. Monica is a great wife; she's just not a great parent. I am."

"But, Chelsea—"

"That's enough."

Mia sighed. "Okay, I'll shut up."

"Good. Let's eat, I'm starving."

"Did you make the chicken wreath?"

Chelsea's mother's recipe of juicy chicken salad wrapped inside a warm croissant wreath had been a revelation to Mia since the first time she'd tried it. She'd grown up in a salmon-and-brown-rice kind of house. Her mother had called mayonnaise *the devil's dairy.*

"You know it," Chelsea answered over her shoulder.

"Hi, River," Mia said.

He stood in the kitchen so pale that he was slightly purple, his long limbs hanging off him like question marks.

"Hey."

Mia couldn't believe he was taller than his mother now. The dudes would be giant dudes too soon. Her shoulders slumped.

Day by day, and not a second more, Mia Macher. Do you hear me?

"Are you excited for your mom's chicken wreath?" Mia asked River. "I know I am."

"Gross," said River.

Chelsea had called her from Publix on Rosh Hashanah once when he was a toddler:

Where the fuck's the challah? she had blubbered, Muzak playing faintly in the background.

They're out of challah! What do I do?

For years it had been the only thing he would eat.

"What do you eat these days?" she asked him now. Sunlight illuminated the very faint mustache growing along his upper lip.

"Hot dogs," he answered.

"Cool," she said.

"Listen, I have bigger battles to fight," Chelsea announced from the sink.

"No judgment," lied Mia.

The back door off the kitchen opened, and Monica walked in. She was a tiny woman, the kind of woman who could live in a pocket.

"Mia!" she announced. A tiny woman with a giant voice. She

crossed through the kitchen toward her and then stopped abruptly. "I want to hug you, but I can't."

"Covid," said Mia. "This sucks."

"Fucking Covid," agreed Monica. "That's why I'm here. My office just shut down, can you believe it?" Monica was a partner at her law firm. "I have to work here now, in the middle of all this." She flailed about wildly, reminding Mia of a hamster on its wheel.

"No," said Chelsea. "Seriously?"

"Seriously."

"You're going to be here?" asked River, grimacing. "All of the time?"

"Oh God, it's awful," said Monica. "And yes. It's only a matter of days before the whole world shuts down, River, including your school. Strap on your seat belts, folks." She turned to Mia. "What are you even doing here? Where are the dudes?"

"Jersey. I got the last flight out, apparently."

"Jesus," murmured Chelsea.

"I'm driving back tomorrow," said Mia. "With Judy."

"In your wildest dreams, could you ever imagine this?" asked Monica. She sliced into the wreath and cut herself a tiny portion. "This is the stuff of science fiction movies."

"And yet it's real," said Chelsea.

"I don't know why I'm not freaking out," said Monica.

"Shock," offered Mia.

It was the same way she had felt when her husband had died. Acceptance was easier than grief. Anything was easier than grief.

CHAPTER 17

"Hey, hey, it's the famous novelist!" Judy shouted as Mia pulled into her childhood driveway.

"What the—" mumbled Mia.

Three women including Judy sat in a semicircle of lawn chairs, and Mia did not like the looks of it one bit.

One, two, three, her mother's voice told Mia as she got out. *Be nice. Be gracious. Keep it to yourself.*

"Hi," she said weakly, climbing out of Chelsea's minivan.

The women were in their seventies, like Judy. One was draped in pearls; the other was wearing a *Wine O'Clock* T-shirt. Judy wore what she always wore: linen.

"Mia!" said Judy as she struggled to get out of her flimsy chair.

"You can do it, can't you, Judy? I'm telling you, you have to start going to Tai-Chi with me. It really makes a difference," said Pearls.

"I'm up, I'm up!" Judy declared breathlessly. "Hi."

"Hi, Judy," said Mia. "What's all this?"

"Well, you said that you would be coming over at four, so I

thought, *Wouldn't it be nice to call over my book club for an impromptu chat?* I thought you might like that. We've all read your books, you know."

Mia did not in fact like it at all. She had two hours before her reading, which was still on, according to her publicist, who was now working from her studio apartment in Queens. New York City had closed down, but Mia's reading would go on? It didn't make any sense. Mia would show up, of course, but it didn't make any sense.

"Okay, but only for a half hour or so," said Mia. "I have to get ready and then get Chelsea's car back to her."

"Oh, sure, sure!" said Wine O'Clock. "We won't keep you long. I have my questions right here!" She dug in her bag to procure a numbered list.

"Can I get a drink from inside?" Mia asked.

"I made you your own tumbler!" Wine O'Clock declared proudly. "With a lid!" She pulled it out of her red travel cooler and threw it in Mia's direction, where it landed with an impressive thud at her feet.

Mia was painted in gold across the front, against a pink glitter background. Mia had not seen anything less *her* in her life.

"Thank you," she said. "I love it."

"It's filled with ice-cold Chardonnay," said Judy proudly. Mia nodded and sat down in an empty lawn chair, which sunk into the damp grass under her weight.

"So," said Pearls. "Your book is sad."

"But also inspiring," said Wine O'Clock.

"But mostly sad," said Pearls again.

Mia took a giant gulp of her wine.

"Well, what happened was sad and it's a memoir, so?" said Mia.

"I was hoping for more funny anecdotes," said Judy. "You've always been so funny in your books."

"She has," agreed Pearls. "All of your books are funny," she told Mia. "Except this one."

"I thought it was funny sometimes," offered Wine O'Clock. "That part about her friend clogging the toilet at the Shiva? That was funny."

"It wasn't a very funny time?" offered Mia.

Mia's Amazon reviews held steady at fourteen. She checked every morning, and the number wasn't going up. Then again, the world was on the brink of an apocalypse. So.

Day by day?

But it's so hard.

"Maybe you'll be happier when you write your next one," offered Pearls as Mia stood up to leave thirty minutes to the second later; she had set a timer on her phone.

"Maybe you'll meet somebody!" said Wine O'Clock.

"Ladies, thank you again," said Mia. "So much. Now, if you'll excuse me, I have to use the bathroom."

"Number one or number two?" Judy asked.

"Excuse me?"

"I set up a fairly large Mason jar in the backyard for number one," she explained. "Because of Covid."

"And what was your number two plan?" asked Mia. Pearls and Wine O'Clock stared at Judy expectantly.

"Well, I figured I didn't have to worry about that. You're always telling Ira how constipated you are."

"I'm going to pee in the toilet, okay? I'll wear my mask."

The nerve of Judy, inserting herself into Mia's intestines! It killed her that Ira repeated everything Mia said to Judy, but of course he did. That was what couples did. And then to make her pee in the yard—like some kind of hillbilly! Like a guest in her own house!—when she was about to be trapped in a car right next to her. It made no sense. Nothing made any sense.

"Wash your hands!" she called after her.

"Fuck off, Judy," Mia grumbled as she jogged up the two steps to her front door.

Mia would never not feel like a little girl in the house she had grown up in; its wood-paneled walls were like a time machine. It wasn't a big house. A ranch was Mia's best guess, because it was one story and angular, but she didn't really know or care about architectural-house speak. It had a seventies vibe to it too, which made sense since Mia had been brought there from the hospital in 1976, when she was brand-new.

The redbrick floor felt cool against Mia's sock-covered feet as she plodded to the pink-tiled bathroom, the same bathroom that she had gotten her first period in. Her mother had taken her out to Olive Garden to celebrate.

She wandered to the bedroom, her mother's oasis once upon a time, when she had still been alive. If it was a Saturday afternoon, that was where her mother would be—snuggled into her blankets, no fewer than four pillows behind her head with a glass of red wine, a stack of books, and four generous slices of mild Cheddar cheese next to four Ritz crackers and four gherkin pickles on a blue-and-white plate.

When they had moved her mother's bed, Mia had found a fork hiding in the dust.

Mia could see her mother's face, her thick eyelashes and the burst capillary beneath her right eye, like a tiny red semicolon.

She called Ira.

"How was the book club?" he asked, grinning into the screen.

"Talk about getting ambushed."

"That Judy, she gets what she wants, you gotta admire that." There was a twinkle in her father's eye that Mia resented.

"I guess," said Mia. "That still doesn't excuse the fact that I was blindsided, but it was fine. They wanted me to be more funny in my memoir about the tragic death of my husband, so."

"They're nice people, but they're not very smart," said Ira. "I don't know why your mother hangs out with them."

"She's not my mother."

"I didn't say that."

"Yes, you did!"

"No, I didn't."

"Dad, please. I can't."

"Listen, your book is beautiful, but it would have been nice to be mentioned in it. It is a memoir, right?"

"I mentioned you!" Mia had mentioned him exactly once, because the last time she had mentioned him in a book, he hadn't spoken to her for two weeks.

"I'm the video store guy?" he had asked repeatedly. "You have that little regard for your father?" The video store guy Mia had written walked like Ira and talked like Ira but looked like Don Rickles.

"Are you really lecturing me right now about who I chose to put in my memoir? Do you realize how narcissistic and stupid that is?"

"I guess you'll write about me when I die, just like you did with your mother. I can live with that." He paused. "Or die with that."

The day before her mother had died, Mia had asked her, as she floated on a cloud of morphine-induced delirium in the bed next to Mia, if she saw anyone at her bedside.

Anyone from the beyond.

"Mia, I'm so glad you asked me that," her mother had replied quietly, closing her lashless eyes. "So glad."

"Yes, Mom?" Mia had asked, so eager to hear that life was worth living.

"And the answer is—"

More silence. Mia checked to make sure her mother was breathing.

"No," she had barked at last. "Don't be ridiculous."

"She was a piece of work, your mother," Ira told Mia. "She would have been so in love with these dudes, let me tell you." There was a catch to his voice, like it had been snagged on Velcro.

"Where are you?" he asked, composing himself so quickly that Mia wasn't sure it had happened at all. "Are you in my bedroom?"

"Yes."

"Oh, look around for my reading glasses, will ya? I know they're there somewhere."

"Okay."

Mia stood up, and the room spun slightly. She would have to

eat the warm protein bar smooshed into the bottom of her purse, since the reading was in twenty minutes. It was wrapped, at least.

"Good night, Dad," she said. "Where are the dudes?"

"Playing H-O-R-S-E."

"Tell them I love them," said Mia.

"We love you too," said her dad.

CHAPTER 18

 "Well, that was weird," said Mia.

She and Chelsea were sitting outside, in the garden of their usual bar, the bar at which they had first used their fake IDs, home for Thanksgiving their freshman year of college.

"I can't believe not one person showed up," she continued. "Although technically I guess I can, it being a pandemic and all." Mia's reading had been a total bust.

"True," Chelsea said, and took a sip of her beer. "By the way, you better bring some Tupperware in the car with you tomorrow. We're not supposed to pee in gas station bathrooms anymore, I read that this morning. Covid City."

"Gross," said Mia.

"Has this ever happened to you before?" Chelsea asked.

"A pandemic?"

"No, doofus, a no-show?"

"Are you kidding?" said Mia. "I only started reading to people who aren't related to me, like, last year. And I've been at this for a decade."

"It's a tough gig," Chelsea said. "But it's what you were meant to do, I really believe that."

"Thanks, Chelsea," said Mia. "Sometimes I don't know."

"What do you mean? You wrote rap lyrics for us in the ninth grade for fun. And they were good! Of course this is what you were meant to do."

"But I'm not supporting my family."

"Are you in trouble?"

"No, no, I just . . . I dunno."

"What, you think a Tesla would make the dudes happy?"

"They are fascinated by them," said Mia. "They discuss the door at least twice a day. What about you? Are you going back to teaching?"

"I dunno." Chelsea had left her job a few years prior, when Monica had made partner and River had become a full-time career. "I'm an old lady and I still don't know what I want to be."

"You don't miss teaching?"

"I miss having my own thing and the kids, but only my favorites and never the parents; they're the worst. But I don't miss the classroom. Not really, anyway."

"You're not an old lady," said Mia.

"Yeah, well. Sometimes when River is at school I watch *The Crown* in the middle of the day."

"Is that a good show?"

"The best."

"But I'm not into the monarchy."

"You don't think you are, but you are," said Chelsea. "The Diana years, at least."

"Do you want to try something new?" asked Mia.

"Sexually or job-wise?"

"Chelsea Lyon, is that you?"

They looked up to find a woman with one of those dreaded mushroom haircuts, the kind that was shaven short but got progressively longer as it approached the top of her head.

Alison McDonald. Mia couldn't believe it.

Chelsea had grown up going to church, a phenomenon that had blown Mia's Jewish mind. She had only gone to synagogue twice a year, and her parents had had to drag her.

Alison had been a Baptist icon not only because she was the pastor's daughter but because she had driven a red convertible Chrysler LeBaron. She had also told fourteen-year-old Mia and Chelsea over Chick-fil-A waffle fries that her boyfriend had "put it in."

"Wow!" Mia had said. The most she had done was swat at Chad Porter's tongue with her own inside a broom closet. "What's sex like?"

Alison's permed head had jerked back as though she'd been slapped—a horrified expression beneath the shellacked canvas of her jawline.

"He puts it in, but it's not sex!" she explained to Mia.

"But does he take it out?" asked Mia, confused.

"Yes," said Alison.

"And then he puts it back in?" asked Chelsea.

"Yes."

The sheer lunacy of the conversation had stuck with Mia; she had even inserted it into her second novel.

"Mia, is that you?" she asked now, peering into her face just to be sure.

Time had ice-skated around Alison's eyes and mouth, but there was something in her eyes that Mia recognized, an exhaustion she knew firsthand.

"It is," said Mia. "Alison, I would have recognized you anywhere." Mia had studied her as a tween, looking for the secret code to popularity.

"That's sweet of you to say," said Alison.

"How have you been?" asked Chelsea. "How are your parents?"

"They're batshit, just like they always were." Alison cackled. "No, I love 'em, but they drive me nuts. My dad poops in a bag now."

"Oh God," said Mia.

"Yeah. Colon cancer. But it's a miracle he's alive, really. We've been praying."

Mia shifted in her seat. Praying hadn't saved her husband.

"Mia, it is just wild that I am seein' you here tonight. W-I-L-D wild."

"It is?" Mia asked.

"I just finished your book this morning!"

"You did?" Mia was shocked. And touched.

"Girl, you saved my life."

"Get out," said Mia. "I did?"

"Two years ago my husband decided to leave me for some slut in his office. Me and our four kids, can you believe it? Four babies I squeezed out for his ass, and then he abandons me for a newer model."

Mia shook her head.

"That's terrible," said Chelsea. "I'm so sorry."

"Thank you," said Alison. "Me too. You know, we had been to-gether since high school. High school. Can you believe it?"

"That's a long time," said Mia.

"And I loved him," continued Alison. "It had never even occurred to me that I would be a divorcée in my forties. Like, what? Me?"

Chelsea nodded in sympathy.

"Mia, your book. It was like you were sittin' inside my soul. That kind of heartbreak, you can't make it up." She searched Mia's masked face with her spider lashes.

"I mean, I know your husband died and mine is just an asshole, but heartbreak is heartbreak, right?"

She was not right. Death was final. Alison could still see her asshole husband at soccer games.

"Right," she lied. "I'm so glad that my book helped you."

"I was like, if sweet li'l Mia can keep goin', then I can keep goin'. I even underlined passages."

"Thank you for reading it," said Mia. "And I'm just so happy it helped you." Mia was. If Alison was one, there had to be at least a few others, and that felt like a gift.

A bedraggled band began to play on the makeshift stage.

"I love this band," Alison announced. "Do y'all love them too?"

"Never heard them before," said Chelsea. "Who are they?"

"The Dingy Dads."

Mia squinted in the dark night, trying to determine whether she knew any of them. The bassist looked like her crush from fourth grade plus thirty pounds and probably was. Atlanta was a big city but felt small.

"I'll be right back," Alison told them. "Y'all want anything from the bar?"

"No thanks," said Chelsea.

"Alison McDonald can read. Who knew?" said Mia as she walked away.

"Be nice," said Chelsea.

"I know," said Mia. "I'm actually really moved."

Divorce and widowhood were nothing at all alike, but the fall-out was a lot of the same. Both of them were living lives they had never envisioned for themselves. Both of them had to still see the good in a universe that had cruelly dismantled all their plans, not to mention make a new plan. It was hard.

"How are your parents, by the way?" Mia asked Chelsea.

"Fine," said Chelsea. "Old. Still pretending that Monica is my friend."

"No!"

"Yes."

"How do you deal with that?"

"I don't," said Chelsea. "I'm not going to change them. And Monica doesn't care. At least they acknowledge her, which is more than I can say for her parents."

"How do you do it? It's unforgivable, their stupidity."

"Yeah, but it's generations of stupid we're talking about here. I'm not going to change them. All I care about is River having grandparents, which he does. They dote on him."

"I just don't understand it," said Mia. "What kind of God won't let people love who they want to love? That's not God. I thought Christianity was supposed to be about grace."

"It's more about fear," explained Chelsea. "I feel sorry for them, really."

"You're too nice," said Mia. "Maybe you should start your own church."

"I've thought about it," said Chelsea. "There are a lot of couples like us who feel abandoned by their religion. But just the idea of it is so overwhelming. Where would I even start?"

"Make an outline."

"You and your outlines," said Chelsea. "I still have that one you made for me in middle school."

"You don't!"

"Of course I do. Roman numeral one: eyeliner."

Mia laughed. Wasn't it something to be exactly the same person, thirty-one years later?

The band launched into a song suddenly, one that Mia knew. It was a Green Day song.

"Hey, y'all, I just want to dedicate this song to the coolest woman I know!" Alison screeched into the microphone. The outside crowd of ten or so leaned toward the stage, waiting.

"Mia Macher! I know your husband is lookin' down on you from heaven, and I know that he's proud of you, honey!"

"Oh my God," said Chelsea.

"What is happening?" asked Mia.

"It can't be," said Chelsea.

"It is," said Mia.

It was a Green Day song; a song that Mia remembered from college. Mia couldn't think of anything more ridiculous than dedicating it to a widow at a bar, but she was the widow, and it was happening to her.

"Another turnin' point, a fork stuck in the road," Alison began, her Southern twang turning it into a country song.

"Let's go," said Chelsea, chugging the rest of her beer. But Mia was already gone.

"Is IT OKAY to laugh?" Chelsea asked Mia in the parking lot.

"Of course it's okay to laugh," said Mia. "You have to laugh, or else you're screwed."

And so they did, climbing into Chelsea's car in hysterics. Mia was mortified, but she was also entertained: Alison's trademark impression. Laughing felt good. She made a vow to do more of it.

"You're so brave," said Chelsea as they drove away "You always have been. From the first moment I met you."

"In a turquoise terry-cloth romper and jelly sandals," said Mia. "Chelsea, I'm sorry I came in here judging your marriage like I did. I just want the best for you is all."

"But your best is not my best," Chelsea told her gently. "We're different people; we always have been, Mia. That's why we're friends. Your marriage is not like mine, and that's okay."

"Was," said Mia. "And I know that. I'm just talking about you giving yourself a break, the same way you just asked me to. You put all this pressure on yourself to be a power parent to River when you have a willing partner to help you shoulder the load. Why would you do that to yourself when you don't have to?"

"It doesn't feel like a job to me, Mia. I don't resent Monica for stepping aside and letting me handle our son. I actually am grateful to her for exactly that. Mothering is my purpose. It's the only thing that feels exactly right. I'm sure it's wrapped up in the way I was parented, or not parented, and maybe that's not great, but it's the best I can do."

"If he's your purpose, what's Monica's?" asked Mia.

"She's the breadwinner. She's the trip planner. She does the laundry. That's how we work. River's not a typical kid. Why do you assume that he would benefit from a typical two parent setup?"

"But what if Monica dies? How could you handle what she handles if you have no idea how it's done? If your duties are so purposefully separate? What if you die? She would be lost with River."

"Neither of us is going to die any time soon, Mia. Statistically it's impossible."

"What?"

"Widows make up seven percent of the population. In my circle of people, it can only happen once statistically. You're the once."

"No wonder I hate math," said Mia.

Mia thought all the time about how much better off the dudes would be if their father was still alive. There was no question. And yet, Chelsea was right. Her marriage was not Mia's marriage. Her history was not Mia's history.

"Okay. I'll leave you alone," said Mia.

"Oh, please don't leave me alone. I couldn't bear it."

"That's not what I meant."

"Good," said Chelsea.

MIA LAY ON the blow-up mattress that Judy had set up for her in the garage and tried to get over the fact that she was sleeping in her garage. Outside. In the distance, an owl hooted.

"You okay?" Judy called from the back door of the house.

"I'm fine," said Mia.

She approached in the wet grass. Mia threw an arm over her eyes.

"Are you sure? I brought out another blanket."

"I'm sure."

"Maybe this was dramatic of me," she said, shining her flashlight directly into Mia's face. "I mean, we are going to share the front seat of the car for thirteen hours."

"That's what I said, Judy, but go ahead and do you."

"Oh, I don't know what to think!" yelled Judy abruptly. Mia had never heard Judy raise her voice before. "We wouldn't even be in this mess if you hadn't needed his help."

"Are you saying that this is my fault?" said Mia.

"I am most certainly not saying that," said Judy defiantly. She was slightly out of breath. "I am simply saying that your father dropped everything to help you, so we need to drop everything and help him. Safely. Because we love him. Well, I do, anyway."

Mia sat up and yanked at her comforter, exposing her bare legs to the brisk night air.

"What are you saying?" she asked Judy.

"I'm saying that you love him when it's convenient for you."

Mia wrestled herself off the air mattress and walked over to

Judy. She had two and a half inches on her, and she wanted Judy to know it.

"You don't know anything about my relationship with my father. You think you know, but you have no idea." A glob of Mia's saliva landed right on Judy's moisturized cheek.

"You've been terrible to me for six years," Judy told her. "I suffer no fools, especially myself. Do you think for one minute that I thought your father wanted me for my supple thighs? Or my world-renowned cooking? He needed a body. So did I."

"How romantic," said Mia.

"That's how we started, but that's not where we are now," Judy continued. "We love each other. And you can't stand that because it doesn't serve you. You're a big baby, Mia Macher!"

"Of course I want my father to be happy!" Mia shouted.

"No, you don't. Not if it doesn't have to do with you, you don't."

"I love my dad," she told Judy. "We're the only two left. He's the only one who has known me as a daughter who is still around. Sharing him, and so soon after she was gone, that was tough. An orangutan could understand that."

"I don't get it. Don't you know firsthand how short life is? Shouldn't he be happy in his? Come inside, for God's sake, so we can stop screaming at each other in public."

"I'm not coming inside," answered Mia.

"Mia, your mother made Ira into the man he is today, and I am so grateful." Judy's voice wavered, bending under the weight of her sadness. "The same goes for my first husband. I met him when I was seventeen years old, can you believe that?"

"Yes," said Mia. "My parents met when they were nineteen. It was a different time."

"Isn't it a miracle that either of us would want to start over again? Don't you think that's brave?"

"You didn't even call me when he died," Mia blurted out. "You sent me a Hallmark card."

"I knew that you didn't like me, Mia. You had made that abundantly clear. I haven't been in the business of winning people over for a long time. I didn't want to overstep my bounds; I didn't want you to think that I thought I was your mother."

"And you knew how awful widowhood was and still. You signed your last name, even! Like I wouldn't know who Judy was?"

"You have no idea how intimidating you are, Mia. I didn't want to add to it. I didn't want to set you off. I didn't want to be responsible for that. When I lost my husband, I was like a ticking time bomb. There was so much rage inside of me."

"I wasn't angry," said Mia. "Not then, anyway. I was too sad to be angry."

"I should have called you," said Judy. "I was a coward."

"And I was a bitch," said Mia. "I'd convinced myself that it was on my mom's behalf, but I know now that it had nothing to do with her. Just like this book tour wasn't about the book."

"It wasn't?" asked Judy.

"No. It was supposed to be about my friends, but I'm not even sure that's true. I barged into their lives spouting advice that they didn't even want. Turns out I was talking to myself the whole time."

"Well, of course you were," said Judy. "The line between you and them is very thin. Translucent, even. I saw you with them at the funeral, the way they held you up. I was jealous. I've never had friends like that."

Mia was tired down to her toes.

"Come inside," said Judy again.

And so Mia did.

CHAPTER 19

Mia stared at the ceiling of her childhood room. She had had the dream again, about her husband with his new girlfriend, although this time she was spared from seeing her.

She sighed and kicked off her covers, rubbed her eyes. Thirteen hours on the road with Judy. Mia sat up for a moment and then lay back down, pulling the covers up and over her head. She rubbed her feet against the cool, crisp cotton.

"Mom, can you believe that my husband died?" she whispered into her makeshift tent. "Can you believe that I write books? That the dudes depend on me? For everything?"

Mia heard Judy clomp by her door. It was time to get up.

There was a sliver of hope in Mia's heart after last night, and that was not nothing.

Slowly Mia washed her face and brushed her teeth; she used the toilet and pulled her clothing out of her suitcase, along with her travel steamer, which she never packed without.

Mia loved to steam; she loved to turn a wrinkled blob back into a shirt with a few foggy passes. Nothing else was that easy and that tangibly rewarding. Mia liked looking nice; she had been taught to care by her mother, and so she did.

As the steamer heated up, Mia walked to her closet. On the top shelf, which Mia could reach only by standing on three shoe boxes precariously stacked, were her journals. She pulled them down. They were inside a discarded moving box she had marked *SCHOOL* as a decoy for her parents, especially Ira—he was unapologetically nosy. She set it on the bed.

"Mia!" Judy called through the door. "Do you want breakfast? We have to get on the road if we want to make it by nine." It was 5:04 A.M.

"No thank you, just coffee!" Mia yelled back. "I'll be out in a minute."

Her steamer began to spit, and Mia dutifully tended to her jeans and shirt, up and down and side to side, until they looked brand-new.

She returned to the box.

Four journals spanning her years of eight to eighteen. Mia thought of the dudes and how quickly time was passing, how fleeting childhood was.

Day by day, Mia.

She plucked one from the stack, turned it over in her hands. It was a Ramona Quimby diary. Her first.

How do your parents make you feel? the diary had asked eight-year-old Mia.

Mad, she had written. *Sometimes.*

She picked up a lavender diary next, from her senior year of high school, thumbing through the pages of unrequited crushes and diet plans. It was so hard to be a girl.

She rooted around in the box for the last journal she had kept; the one that recounted her meeting her husband when he was just her subway crush. When they had lived two blocks from each other in Brooklyn; their separate apartments nestled into brownstones; lights on in the windows as they texted each other from their futons. Mia had never been in love before. She had obsessed over and cried about other men, but was never in love.

She flipped to a page, just to see.

This is my journal, she had written in her cramped cursive. *And because it's mine alone, I will write something here that no one can know. I'm in love with Subway Crush. He makes me happy. Really happy. I want to be his girlfriend. Meet his family. Make him macaroni and cheese. Whatever happens, I am grateful for him here. Now. In this moment.*

Mia looked up from the journal, her eyes wet. Day by day. Even then.

Mia placed it back in the box, climbed on top of the stool, and slid it back into place onto the highest shelf in the closet. Wasn't it something?

Wherever you went, there you were. She had lived. She had loved. And she had lost.

"Oh, baby girl," she whispered. "You're so much stronger than you could possibly know. You're not going to believe it."

"Mia, honestly!" Judy called through the door.

"Coming!" she yelled.

Packing the celadon-green Corolla with Judy had been a passive-aggressive game of killer chess. Every time Mia slid in a bag, Judy would cross-check her with a pillow or a lone container of Metamucil.

Finally, they had agreed on the logistics of their shared interior, and after arguing Waze versus Google Maps for a solid twenty minutes in the sleet (obviously it was Waze—*Do you want to get there in thirty hours or thirteen hours, Judy?*), they hit the road with Mia at the wheel.

The highway stretched ahead of Mia as wide and open as she had ever seen it. On the radio, a panel of reporters droned on about masks and droplets.

It occurred to Mia, for the first time, really, that they were not going to come out of the pandemic any time soon. That she and the dudes were going to be completely alone for a very long time. Someone was saying that it would be a year before a vaccine was even green-lit.

"What do you think?" asked Judy from the passenger seat, pulling Mia out of her Bermuda Triangle of despair.

"Sorry, what? I didn't hear you," said Mia.

She glanced at Judy, who had a book of crossword puzzles open on her lap. A pair of wire-rimmed glasses magnified her brown eyes dramatically, giving her an owl-like quality. Being nice to Judy would involve such a rerouting of their relationship. She was exhausted just thinking about thinking about it. But she would do it. It would be worth it.

"Do you think the *New York Times* has the best crossword puzzles?" she asked Mia.

"Oh man, I don't know," said Mia. "I'm not a crossword puzzle kind of person."

"Really?" asked Judy. "I would think that it would be an excellent way to increase your vocabulary. As a writer and all."

Rationally, Mia knew that Judy's intent was not malicious, but it felt that way.

"Oh no, I can tell by your expression that you don't like what I just said," said Judy. "I didn't mean that as an insult, I swear. You're a terrific writer."

"Thank you," said Mia. "I don't know why I get so defensive. Old habit, I guess."

"I've read all of your books, you know," Judy told Mia. "I didn't want to like your writing, but I did. I do."

"Dad told me that you're a voracious reader. My mom was too."

"I know," said Judy. "Ira has told me all about her, but who was she to you?"

"Honest. My mom was never one to hold back. If she didn't like you, you knew."

"You don't say," said Judy.

Mia smiled. "She loved to read. She was very smart. She was beautiful. But she wasn't nice."

"Nice is overrated," said Judy.

"But it's really not," argued Mia. "When my husband died, the niceness of people—it astounded me. It kept me and the dudes alive, really. It taught me how to be a better person, other people's niceness."

"I always thought nice people were dumb," said Judy. "But that's not true. My first husband wasn't nice. But he was depressed, so?"

"Oh, I'm sorry." The sun was beginning its ascent into the pink-and-lavender sky. "That must have been very hard."

"He killed himself, you know."

"Oh my God," said Mia, glancing at Judy, who looked straight ahead. "I didn't know. My dad never told me."

"I don't like to talk about it," said Judy.

"What happened? What about your sons?" Judy had three.

"They don't know either. I told them it was a heart attack."

"Oh Judy," said Mia. The sky was blue now. All along the highway the trees were budding, opening up to the possibility of spring.

"They were all out of the house by then," she explained. "Grown-ups. He waited.

"He turned on the car and just sat in the garage," said Judy as she wrote the word *test* across four boxes in the middle of the page.

"I'm sorry," said Mia. "That's awful."

"It sure was," said Judy. She looked at Mia, finally. "I found him, you know."

"Jesus, Judy."

"I didn't want our boys to carry any anger toward their father, so I fudged the facts a little."

"But that's a lot to carry on your own," said Mia.

"I manage. And it's much easier with your father around."

Judy pulled a Ziploc of bagels with cream cheese and a container of apple slices out of the black cooler at her feet.

Bagels and apple slices had been her parents' go-to road travel meal since Mia was a kid, lying in the back of their station wagon and playing Willie Nelson on her brown Fisher-Price tape player. Now it was Judy's too.

Virginia Is for Lovers, a red-and-black welcome sign proclaimed as Mia drove past it.

"By the time I met your father, I had been alone for eight years," said Judy. "My sons were gone, and it was just me, rattling around our big house where my husband had killed himself. I never imagined that I could meet someone new. Not until I did."

"You met at the pet store, right?" she asked Judy.

"We sure did. I was looking into getting a Betta fish and so was he. Now, you know your father, won't spend a dime, so we started talking because I saw him leaning toward the fishbowl rather than the tank. No fish can live in a bowl. That's only on television, in case you didn't know that."

"I do know that." Mia thought of Squiggly, swimming on against all the odds, reassuring the dudes that she would be okay.

"He did end up springing for the tank."

"To impress you," said Mia.

"Well, it worked. I took Patsy Cline home, and he got Paul Newman. He also got my number. The rest is history, I guess. I may not know everything, but I do know that your father is the least depressed person I've ever met. The odds of him offing himself are pretty much nil, so that's good for my PTSD."

"He would never," said Mia. "He likes himself too much."

"He really does," agreed Judy. "And he likes me."

"It doesn't bother you, being his second wife?" asked Mia.

"No, not really," said Judy. "It's because of your mother that he's perfect for me. Barbara did all the heavy lifting.

"Do you want to meet anyone new?" Judy asked.

Mia grimaced and then got mad at herself for grimacing, because if she was lucky, she had about forty-five or so more years to go, and that was a long time to go without meeting someone new.

"I just want to stay alive long enough to see the dudes get settled," she told Judy. "Once upon a time I dated the free world, but that doesn't even feel like my life anymore. That's what this book tour was supposed to be about—reconciling my past with my future. A roman à clef except you know, I'm forty-three." A bug splat on the windshield in front of her.

"Did you get any reconciling done?" asked Judy.

"Not really. I got a pandemic breathing down my neck instead."

"Well, there you go," said Judy, biting into an apple slice.

"Hey, Judy?" asked Mia.

"Yes?" She brushed nonexistent crumbs off her lap.

"How come you never tried to be friends with me?"

"You've got to be kidding me," said Judy.

"What?"

"You were thirty-eight years old when Ira and I married, not nine. A grown woman with a child of her own! It was ridiculous. And I did try. A little in the beginning. You gave me nothing. I suppose if I was a different kind of person I would have tried harder. But I'm not, so? It wasn't a picnic for my boys either, you know. But they got over it. You have to remember that I married

Hank right out of college. I had never been alone in my life, and it turns out that I don't like it very much. By the time I met Ira, I was just so damn tired, Mia. I wanted someone to take care of me again, that's the truth. And Ira likes to take care of me, God bless him."

Mia nodded reverently. That first summer, when the afternoon stretched on for hours and she and her husband, her boyfriend at the time, rode the sun to bed on their bicycles through Brooklyn every night, Mia had felt taken care of for the first time in her life. The way he detached his bike lock from his waist and strung it through the spokes of both of their wheels before bolting both of them to the fence—his care for her was love in motion.

"You're very lucky to have the girlfriends that you do," Judy told Mia. "You really take care of each other. I never had friends like that."

"What about the book club?"

"Oh please," said Judy. "It's not like that."

Mia thought of George, she thought of Rachel, and she thought of Chelsea. They recharged her, even when she didn't feel like being recharged. All she wanted was to do the same for them.

"And you have those wonderful dudes," said Judy. "I bet you don't have time to be lonely."

"But loneliness isn't a consequential feeling, I don't think. If you're lonely, you're lonely, no matter who's around."

It had been like that in New York for Mia. At first. Everywhere she went: the subway, the sidewalks, even her tiny apartment had been crowded with people, and still it was the loneliest Mia had ever felt. She had wanted to move home.

"Yes, come home," her healthy mother had said. "We'll figure it out."

"If you come home, I'll kill you," Ira had told her. "Don't you give up, Mia."

"Kill me?"

"You can get through this. I know you'll get through this. What did I tell everyone you were going to be when you grew up? When you were a baby, what did I say?"

"The first female president of the United States."

"So? Let's go already."

"Dad. I'm miserable."

"Of course you are. You don't like your job, you're not writing, and you put on weight. You can change all those things, Mia. And you will. In New York. Not here."

And Mia had.

"Judy?"

"Yes, Mia?"

"I think if you had waited a couple years to marry my dad, I wouldn't have been such a bitch to you."

"Woulda, coulda, shoulda," said Judy.

Mia looked at the dashboard clock. Eight hours to go.

CHAPTER 20

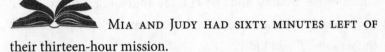 MIA AND JUDY HAD SIXTY MINUTES LEFT OF their thirteen-hour mission.

Mia had always hated to drive. She hadn't had a car in high school, her parents having looked at her like she was from outer space when she had asked for one, and then who needed one in Boston or New York? Mia much preferred walking. She was an excellent walker.

When she had brought her husband home to meet her parents, he hadn't believed her that she couldn't drive.

"You're so dramatic!" he had said. "Get in, you're driving us downtown."

Forty-five minutes of near-death merges and a parallel park that required an intervention from a pedestrian later, Mia had shakily removed the key from the ignition.

"I guess you weren't kidding," he had said, white as a sheet.

"I know I have to drive, but I will never actually enjoy it," she would tell him a few years later, when she didn't shake every time her hands held the steering wheel.

Now she did.

What in the world was her life going to look like now, in a pandemic? If it was hard with help at the ready and school, what did harder even look like?

Day by day.

"Do you ever have dreams about your husband?" Judy asked her. It was cold now. Mia had turned on the heater, and it smelled like a toaster in the car.

"I do, but they're terribly disappointing," she answered. "He's with another woman, and I wake up so angry. I hate them."

"Probably your subconscious trying to make some sense out of the senseless," said Judy.

"I guess. But it's just so mean."

"Your father tells me all the time about the dream he had. The one with your mother."

"That one's a doozy," said Mia. "It's the answer to everything, if you let yourself believe it."

If Mia believed his dream, she could believe in anything, really. That was a lot of pressure on a broken heart.

"What am I going to do during this pandemic?" she asked Judy. "Everyone is too terrified to be nice. You can't even hug people anymore."

"It's going to be very hard," said Judy. "For you. Not so much for us. We barely go anywhere." She sighed. "Although I will miss the library."

"Being a widow at my age is so lonely," Mia admitted. "No one else gets it."

"I get it," said Judy.

"Sometimes I worry that I'll never be fun again," said Mia. "Not really, anyway. Even when I'm happy, I'm sad."

"You have to redefine fun," said Judy. "There's nobility in being smashed to bits and seeking joy anyway. It's a challenging fun, but maybe that makes it more worthwhile. I certainly had to redefine it when I fell for your father. It's heroic in a way, don't you think?"

Mia considered Judy's point of view. In a sense, Mia had the chance now to be the kind of protagonist she wrote about. The hero's journey was the core of every story worth telling.

"I do," she told Judy.

Mia turned onto her street now, at last, her heart pounding in her ears, her palms sweating. If she hadn't known better, she would have said that her breasts were leaking, that was how intensely her maternal overdrive had kicked in.

She pulled into the driveway, and the brakes screeched. She almost forgot to turn the car off as the dudes tumbled out of the front door and toward her, tripping over their feet to get to her.

"Mom!" they yelled, and nuzzled into her.

Her puppies.

Their puppies.

"I really missed you!" yelled her younger, kissing her neck repeatedly, like an overzealous French lover.

"I told you that you would make it!" her elder whispered into her ear.

"I always do," Mia whispered back.

Ira appeared in the doorway, his suitcase packed.

"You made it!" he cried. "Very good, girls. Very good."

"Ira!" Judy called out, and took his hand. Mia and the dudes unwound themselves from each other and looked up at the two of them.

"Get that silly suitcase unpacked," she told him. "You and I are staying."

ACKNOWLEDGMENTS

I STARTED WRITING THIS BOOK JUST BEFORE COVID LOCKED US all away in March 2020. I had been a single mother for two years at that point, but never alone. Friends were always just a phone call away, ready to pick me up something at the grocery store or swoop in to take the dudes for an hour or two so I could breathe.

We also had school. God bless school.

That all changed with Covid of course, and in between ferrying snacks upstairs to my nine year old and fetching paper for my five year old, I wondered if I was going to write ever again. I can do pretty much anything else with the dudes around, but I can't write. It requires all of me.

My mother, Sue, and brother Brenner saved us. Four afternoons a week they would come over and sit with the dudes so that I could write this book. Which I did. In the garage.

And we're not talking a she-shed. It's a garage filled with nuts, bolts, rattraps, wires, and an old IKEA dinner table posing as a desk next to a deep freeze filled with waffles and Trader Joe's pizzas. That's where I wrote the first draft of *Fun Widow*.

I could not have done it without their help and I want to thank them from the bottom of my heart. And they didn't just sit with the dudes either; they taught them too. Uncle Brenner especially. I love you both. Thank you for showing me what family is.

I want to thank Nurit and Karen too, for being the best in-laws, Savta, and Tia we could ever hope for. I hate that we're on this path of grief, but so grateful that we're walking it together. You inspire and teach me every day.

Thank you to Lauren, Sarah, Gina, Justine, Andrea, Joel, and Karen for listening. I was a mess.

Thank you to the wonderful teachers at Winnona Park and Talley Street. Without you I could not have written the second, third, and fourth drafts of this book and *oooowee* did I need to.

Which brings me to my gratitude for my kick-ass agent, Jess Regel, and smart-as-a-whip editor, Lucia Macro. Thank you for your patience. Thank you for your suggestions. Thank you for pushing me to do better because you knew I had it in me.

Thank you to my copy editor, Andrea Monagle. Holy cow, are you good! Wow.

Thank you to my Zoedies: Lauren, Sarah, Steel, Iulia, Elizabeth, Emily, Sheps, Alice, Mike, Audrey, Greg, Dana, and Sooz. You're the inspiration here. This time around, we're going everywhere. Bali, anyone?

And finally, thank you to the loves of my life: Ari and Lev. When you were tiny, Gima told me our relationship was *like a love affair*. He was right. I'm crazy about you for so many reasons and sincerely feel like the luckiest Ema alive. Your Aba would be astounded by the beautiful humans you've become but not surprised. You were special right from the start.

About the author

2 Meet Zoe Fishman

About the book

4 A Conversation with Zoe Fishman

11 Reading Group Guide

Insights,
Interviews
& More . . .

Meet Zoe Fishman

Karen Scaham

ZOE FISHMAN is the 2020 Georgia Author of the Year. She is the bestselling author of five previous novels and has won several awards, including *Booklist*'s "Top 10 Books of the Year" and an Indie Next pick. She's been featured on *City Lights* with Lois Reitzes, and in *Publishers Weekly* and the *Atlanta Jewish Times*, among other publications. Her essays have been published in the *New York Times*'s "Modern Love" column,

the *Atlanta Journal-Constitution*, and
Modern Loss. Zoe was the director of
the Decatur Writers Studio and a visiting
writer at SCAD Atlanta. She lives in
Decatur with her two sons. ∾

A Conversation with Zoe Fishman

Q: You've been very candid about the fact that this book is about as meta as meta can get. What's it like to write a book about an author promoting a memoir and then to actually be an author promoting a memoir thinly veiled as fiction?

A: Weird. Scary. But also empowering. I just want to clarify that although Mia is essentially me—and some of her experiences, and all of her missing of her husband and who she used to be are mine—the other characters are a mix of imagination and real life.

Right after my husband died, I wrote *Invisible as Air*, which was the exact right book for me to write at that time. It was about grief, but it wasn't my grief, and it was good to have that distance while at the same time having what I hope was the proper empathy.

After it was published, I submitted an essay about my husband and two young sons to the *New York Times*'s "Modern Love" column, and, to my great delight and disbelief, it was accepted and published in December of 2020. Readers' responses were humbling and beautiful and so very kind. I think a big reason for that was because my writing came straight from my heart.

I wanted to do more of that kind of writing, and I started to imagine the idea of a memoir, but the truth is that publishing is a business. No one was going to buy my memoir as a relatively unknown author was the message (albeit in a nice way) upon my asking, and so *Fun Widow* was born.

A very true part of this novel is the incredible friendships Mia has. My girlfriends rallied around me and my sons in a way that absolutely moved me to my core. Without them, I don't know how I would have made it through that first year. Not only did I have boots on the ground here in Decatur, Georgia, where I live, but every month someone would fly in and hang with the three of us for a couple days—leaving their own jobs and families behind to bring some light to mine. To take the boys on adventures and for fast food and sodas—whatever they wanted!—so that I could breathe. Their kindness profoundly shaped who my sons are today, in the best way possible. They are kind and thoughtful humans despite the tragedy that befell them.

So even as there were many moments and still are during which I belittle myself for having the audacity to think that my experience is important enough to share on such a grand platform, ultimately it's a tribute to the selflessness of others and how it became my life raft during a very difficult time. ▸

A Conversation with Zoe Fishman
(continued)

Q: *Your novel pulls back the curtain on the book tours most of us imagine for authors. Was that your intention initially?*

A: Yes. So many people seem to think that every author, no matter what their status, is rolled out a red carpet and flown all over the country to engage with readers as soon as their book goes on sale. While that may be the case for the bestsellers among us, it is certainly not the case for the majority. Budgets are not what they used to be—if they ever were at all? Maybe the grand author tour has forever been a myth, I don't really know.

What I do know is that, just like Mia, almost all of my bookstore appearances have been the result of networking with friends and with their hometown bookstores. There's only so much publicity you can do if your readership doesn't guarantee a bustling audience, and I appreciate and understand that.

In the best cases, I've been able to wrangle an appearance at what is always a wonderful store run by wonderful book-loving people who are gracious enough to allow me to speak about my book, but in some cases it just doesn't work out. Or two people show up and I feel like a total ass for wasting the booksellers' time.

I also wanted to highlight the beauty of the Q & A format at bookstore events. It's so much better and easier in my opinion to have someone to engage with onstage as opposed to boring the pants off your audience with a monologue. The difference is night and day, at least for me.

Q: You wrote the first draft of **Fun Widow** *during the Covid lockdown, when both of your sons were home from school full-time and, later, for half of each weekday. What was your process like?*

A: Oof. Just remembering those endless months makes me shudder. What a tough time to be a single, working parent. I've always been a disciplined writer, not for any reason other than that I love it and I know that if I don't show up every day, my focus is screwed. But 2020 was hard.

My mother and brother, who both very graciously moved to Atlanta after my husband died, came over a few afternoons a week to sit with the boys as they schooled and snacked. So many snacks! God, it was awful.

I would gather up my laptop, my notebook, my pencil, and my glasses and retreat to my backyard garage, which is more of a shed than a garage since it's filled with the overflow of our lives and not my car. And by shed, I don't mean she-shed. I set up a table and some chairs next to the deep-freeze, rolled up the door, swept the cockroach carcasses and spiderwebs out of the way, and wrote ▶

A Conversation with Zoe Fishman
(*continued*)

for three hours while they helped the boys with virtual school.

Technically, I was writing, since I was following my outline and moving my fingers across the keyboard, but wow. My first draft was horrible. My first drafts are always horrible but this one took the cake. Initially, I had Mia on a road trip. Don't ever try to write a road trip when you are in lockdown, or maybe don't try to write a road trip ever. Filling the silence in the car in between stops was painful. Or at least my attempt at it was.

My editor and agent were very kind after reading that draft, but they were also like: *no*. At that point, I think it was summer? The boys were masked but in camp and finally: I had my house and relative sanity back. Through the fall and beyond, I rewrote the whole thing and will never take school or teachers for granted ever again.

Q: What was your favorite scene to write?

A: I have to say that the book's ending, when Mia returns to the dudes, was my favorite. It was so triumphant! So optimistic. So true to how I feel about my commitment to them.

I also very much enjoyed writing the California reading scene, when Mia imagines an audience member taking her to task for capitalizing on her husband's death. That's been my biggest fear with all of my writing concerning his loss: that someone might misinterpret my intentions.

Writing him and us and our family back to life is the greatest gift I could give myself and the most consequential for my mental health. Writing has always been my therapy, but never more so than after his death. I've had to remind myself of that many times throughout this process. Writing is the only way in which I truly heal.

Q: Who was the hardest character for you to write?

A: Judy. I couldn't figure her out at first. Who was she and why would she marry a widower so soon after his wife's passing? And if she was someone who didn't like to be alone, how could I understand her?

I like to be alone; I liked to be alone even when I was married—just to relish the silence. But I thought about Judy, and just how silent her empty house would have been, and just how long the days probably were, and I could understand why Ira would sweep her off of her feet.

I gave her a backstory with her husband's suicide and then I understood her more. The guilt and anger she might feel. Her practicality became three-dimensional in that it was really more of a defense mechanism than anything else. And if you live through ▶

A Conversation with Zoe Fishman
(continued)

that kind of loss, I would imagine that you wouldn't have the time for people's imagined impressions of you. Mia wasn't nice to Judy and so Judy wasn't nice back.

I really enjoyed writing the scenes with those two in Atlanta and in the car, because they're both being so vulnerable, which is an emotion that doesn't come easily for either of them but ultimately bridges their gap, the way shared vulnerability always does.

Q: What's next?

A: I'm toying with the idea of branching out into historical fiction and am especially interested in New York's Gilded Age and the fascinating female criminal masterminds who dominated that era. This would be my first foray into the genre, and although I'm incredibly intimidated by the amount of research a book like this would require, I'm also excited to try something new. 〜

Reading Group Guide

1. What did you think about Mia's grieving process? Was it as you imagined a widow might feel or different?

2. Who was your favorite character and why? Your least favorite?

3. Did you already know about the realities of book touring for most authors or did you assume that a red carpet was rolled out for each?

4. What did you think about Mia's intentions to fix her friends' marriages as a way of repaying them for all of their many kindnesses in the aftermath of her husband's death? Misguided? Masochistic? A little of both?

5. This book is about relationships: romantic, platonic, and biological. Whose relationship did you most relate to and why?

6. Mia takes her father's ideology to heart and believes that luck isn't real but timing is. What do you think about Ira's belief?

7. The author never names Mia's husband or her sons, choosing to refer to him by his moniker and to them as "the dudes." Did this bother you or could you appreciate her decision? ▶

8. Mia is rude to Judy for most of their relationship, but would you say her behavior was warranted? How would you behave in that situation, if your father remarried less than two years after your mother's death?

9. There are lots of moments in the book where a well-meaning someone says something to Mia about her widowhood that really pisses her off, like "I can't imagine" or "Everything happens for a reason." Have you ever unknowingly said these things to someone who's grieving?

10. Knowing what we now know about that first Covid year, what do you think day-to-day life looked like for Mia, the dudes, Ira, and Judy in New Jersey? ⌒

Discover great authors, exclusive offers, and more at hc.com.